THE PHANTOM ARCHER

Five men and one woman had died horribly. The evidence suggested that all had died at night and, more puzzling, none displayed any signs of external physical damage. No bruising, lacerations or stab marks. And yet the post-mortems had revealed incredible evidence of extensive internal trauma; shattered bones, ruptured livers, severe lung punctures, abdominal damage, and 'bullet-like' injuries to the skull.

Police surgeons were baffled as to the cause of death; it was almost as though they had been repeatedly shot by a low-calibre rifle and then the killer has somehow sealed all the entry and exit wounds. Were these actual murders, and were they the work of one individual, or was a real-life serial killer on the loose?

THE PHANTOM ARCHER

Edmund Glasby

WILDSIDE PRESS

Contents

One

The Phantom Archer

A heavy rain lashed against the windows of Detective Inspector Andrew McGovern's office as he sat in his chair staring pensively at the wall clock, wondering whether or not he had made the right decision in agreeing to the meeting which was scheduled for ten minutes time. He had been based at Kilwinning, a small town on the Ayrshire coast, for three years, having previously served in Glasgow where he had worked his way up through the ranks in the Strathclyde Constabulary. Over the course of his twenty-seven years in the police force he had successfully investigated numerous murder cases and had developed a dour, hard-nosed approach to life in general. There was no denying the fact, however, that the current spate of mysterious deaths had him and his team floundering in the dark.

To date, over the course of the late summer and early autumn, six horrible deaths had occurred. Five men and one woman. The evidence suggested that all had died during the hours of darkness and, more puzzling, none of them displayed any signs of external physical damage. No bruising. No lacerations. No stab marks. And yet, the X-rays and the post-mortems had revealed incredible evidence of extensive internal trauma; perforated scapulae and hip bones, shattered femurs and ulnas, ruptured livers, severe lung punctures and abdominal damage. In three instances there were 'bullet-like' injuries to the skull.

"It's unbelievable, Andy. It's almost as though they've been repeatedly shot by a low-calibre rifle and then the killer has somehow sealed all the entry and exit wounds," had been Vic Morrow, the police surgeon's only explanation. He had gone on to talk about factors such as massive impact cavitation and brain death caused by hydrostatic shock but had been unable to ascertain a definite cause of death. Internal bleeding remained a possibility.

Consequently, it was still debatable as to whether these were actual murders. And whilst McGovern held to the belief that all of this was the work of one individual and that there was a real life serial killer on the loose, there remained that tiny doubt that perhaps these deaths could be ascribed to natural causes. After all, all he had to go on were dead bodies with no obvious connection between them. If it was murder, then how the hell was it being committed? It was this conundrum and the realisation that it couldn't be answered by what he termed 'conventional' means that had finally made him acquiesce to the suggestion of obtaining outside help. Besides, from the information he had researched, baffling as it had first appeared, Paul Lowry had assisted the police once or twice in the past.

* * * *

"Say hello to Mr. Jim Buchanan." Morrow, a small, bespectacled man who preferred the company of the dead to the living, pulled back the humped white sheet to reveal the cadaver's cold and grey face. He dragged the sheet down further, revealing the entirety of the naked, corpulent corpse. A series of neat autopsy scars ran from the groin over the flabby stomach to the gullet. There were several other criss-crossing stitch marks visible on his limbs. "Age fifty-seven. Five-foot-nine. Twenty-two stone, eleven pounds."

McGovern turned to Lowry, disliking what he saw. For whilst McGovern was clean-shaven and in his formal attire, the psychic was scruffy, unkempt and unshaven, his clothes casual and, by the looks of it, unwashed. A typical New Age weirdo, the inspector wouldn't be at all surprised to discover that the man had tattoos and a pierced belly button. There was a living scarecrow look to him, like that of a half-dead rock star. What was more, he was standing there, looking at the corpse, one scrawny finger delving into his left nostril. No doubt if the other hadn't been able to make a living from beguiling folk with his so-called mystical talents he would be lying drunk in a gutter somewhere, he thought judgementally. "This is the latest victim. If there's anything you can tell me I would very much appreciate it. And for God's sake, stop picking your nose and show some respect." Despite having only met the man, whom he reckoned to be in his early thirties, a few minutes ago, based on first impressions he had already reached the view that the other would be of no use whatsoever. He himself did not give much credence to the so-called abilities of psychics, believing them to be nothing more than charlatans who hindered more than assisted the police in their investigations.

With a disgruntled sigh, Lowry removed the offending digit and took a couple of paces towards the body. He reached out, taking one of the lifeless hands in his. Then, closing his eyes, he seemed to go into the initial phases of a meditative trance. His breathing became heavier as he slowly began to move his head from side to side. He began to mumble, his words weird and barely audible as though they were meant for the corpse's ears alone.

McGovern threw the police surgeon an unimpressed glance. The look he received in return mirrored his own. This was bordering on the ludicrous.

A cheek muscle on Lowry's face began to twitch. A low moan escaped his lips as his grip on the dead man's hand tightened.

For one terrible moment McGovern had a mental image of the deceased's eyes flicking open like something out of a horror film—of Mr. Buchanan suddenly animating, sitting upright on the metal slab. Shaking the unsettling vision from his mind, he stared perplexedly at Lowry, wondering how much longer this madness would continue. The spectacle before him certainly ranked amongst one of the strangest things he had ever seen. And it was something that could hardly be explained away as 'in the line of duty' should the press ever get wind of any of this. God alone knew what the dead man's relatives would think.

Suddenly Lowry released the lifeless hand and jerked back, his abrupt actions taking the other two men by surprise. The psychic's eyes were wide and staring and the skin on his face had become several shades lighter. He hadn't appeared too healthy when he had first introduced himself, but now he looked positively sick. "Christ!" He pointed a finger from a hand that was trembling. "Can't you...can't you see? Those wounds."

"What is it? What are you talking about?" Sceptically, McGovern thought that this little bit of melodrama was nothing more than a show. A nice piece of over-acting in order to instil some level of belief in what the other was no doubt about to impart. After all, he could see nothing unusual.

"There are wounds." Lowry indicated numerous places on the body. Looking around, he noticed a magnifying glass resting on a tray filled with surgical equipment and with it, began scrutinising the body anew. "There are holes. Deep holes, perhaps less than an inch in diameter, boring straight into the flesh."

Intrigued, Morrow handed Lowry a black marker pen. "Would you put an 'X' where these wounds are?"

Curious, McGovern watched as the psychic began his spectral autopsy, running his long-fingered hands over the flabby dead flesh, pausing every now and then to put his mark.

"I think that's the lot," said Lowry, having now put nine large black crosses on the corpse. "I daresay that if we flip him over, I'll find more on the other side." Marker pen in hand, he stepped back to allow McGovern and Morrow to turn the body over. "Yes. As I thought. There are several exit wounds. That's of course assuming his attacks came from the front. I'm no expert, so it's hard to be sure." He counted those he could detect. "There are five." He marked them.

"Are you quite sure that the frontal and rear wounds match up? Would you say they were inflicted—?" Morrow began.

"Hang on a moment, Vic," McGowan interrupted. "You're not telling me you've been taken in with all this mumbo-jumbo, have you? All I can see is a stiff that now looks as though it's been turned into a noughts-and-crosses board. Either that or a treasure map with one too many 'Xs'. Now, I'll admit I've read a little about Mr. Lowry's alleged successes in finding missing people and—"

"For your information, I have assisted the police on numerous occasions." It was now Lowry's turn to be argumentative. "I'll admit my track record may not be one hundred percent but there's no doubt my specialised talents have proven invaluable in solving certain cases. May I also remind you that it was *you* who contacted me for help." He gestured to the cadaver. "What I see before me is a dead man riddled with holes. As I said, I'm not a medical expert but there's no doubt in my mind that this man died a very violent death from multiple injuries."

"Assuming you're right, what kind of weapon would you envisage caused such wounds?" asked Morrow. There was a measure of sincerity to his question which McGovern took as a level of acceptance of what Lowry had related. The police surgeon was obviously taking this seriously.

"Hard to say. They could be spear or sword thrusts. A rapier, perhaps? I'd rule out bullets for as far as I'm aware they create a much larger exit wound." The psychic returned the magnifying glass to the tray. "How long's he been dead?" he asked.

Morrow consulted his watch. "Approximately thirty-six hours. Why?"

Lowry grinned. "It's just that I'm fairly confident that with a more recently deceased body I'd get more information."

McGovern tutted his disapproval.

Morrow gazed at the corpse, which now lay face down, making a mental note of where the psychic had placed his 'Xs'. The dead man's stone cold weighty buttocks had the greyish colour of a week-old blancmange. After a moment's consideration, he turned to McGovern. "I know what you're thinking, Andy. But there's no doubt in my mind that our friend here does, dare I say, possess powers that I can't even begin to understand for he's accurately pinpointed the exact locations where there has been an occurrence of internal trauma right down to where excessive bone damage and fragmentation has resulted in the failure of the penetrative 'object' from exiting the body. How he's managed to do this without recourse to my post-mortem report, I don't know."

* * * *

"Well, what do you make of it all, Vic? You seem to have to been taken in by Lowry's little performance." It was several hours later, and McGovern was back in his office going over things with the police surgeon. Also present was his sergeant, Hamish Thom, a stocky, dependable man who had been fully briefed on the morning's developments.

"Somehow, he knew exactly where to indicate the vital trauma regions. I honestly think that had we the other bodies he would have been able to replicate what he did."

"Hmm. Still, it throws very little light on just what's happening."

"I agree, but at least I think we can now rule out death by natural causes. From all indication these were violent homicides."

"Not a weird disease of any kind?" asked McGovern. "A parasitic infestation, maybe? A bad case of worms or something?" He knew it was an absurd question, but things were becoming stranger by the minute and permitting his inquiries to spiral away into the world of the paranormal was not something he was about to let happen, if it could be avoided.

Morrow shook his head. "Nothing I'm aware of."

McGovern sat back, a deeply confused and troubled look on his face. This case was unlike anything he had ever been involved with before. As a pragmatic man who was used to dealing with tangible evidence, he had no real experience of how to even begin tackling this crime—if indeed it was a crime. If, as the police surgeon had implied, the deaths were not natural in origin, then what the hell were they? How were they being committed? No weapon known to man could cause such injuries without leaving signs of external entry. It was impossible. A part of him realised he was edging towards a precipice—the fall beyond descending into the realm of the implausible and the supernatural. Surely there had to be other explanations. But what were they?

For the best part of a minute there was only the sound of the rain outside as the three of them wracked their brains for answers. There seemed little they could do but increase police numbers on the streets and warn the public not to venture out at night unless it was absolutely necessary. Amidst the populace of the town there was noticeable alarm with some, amongst the more superstitious, already attributing the deaths to a demonic agent. Such a belief had originated after the first victim, Duncan Hartwell, a local schoolteacher, had been discovered in the ruins of the old Abbey, his contorted body found slumped over a low wall. The look on his face had been one of sheer horror.

McGovern rose from his chair. He went over to a large street map of the town, the locations where the bodies had been discovered marked by red circles Tacked to it were numerous paper clippings and small photographs. "There doesn't appear to be any pattern to these deaths whatsoever. I think they're completely random. If we assume that we have a serial killer at large, and to be honest with you, I'm still finding that hard to believe, then I think the only thing we can do is step up our patrols. Door-to-door questioning has led us nowhere and we've got next to nothing to go on. Hell, we don't even have a motive as yet although we can rule out theft or anything of a sexual nature."

"I wouldn't raise this if I could think of anything else, but..." Thom hesitated, unsure how to continue.

"Well?" prompted McGovern, preparing himself for things to become even stranger. No doubt the other was going to relate some bedtime ghost story that had been handed down the generations.

"As you know I'm in the Ancient Society of Kilwinning Archers, the oldest archery society in Britain. Annually we hold the papingo shoot up the Abbey tower. Anyway, there's a legend concerning several unexplained fatalities that occurred here way back. I think we're talking at least four hundred years ago in the Sixteenth Century."

"Do you think this is relevant?" McGovern paced back to his chair and sat down.

Thom shrugged his shoulders. "Common sense would tell me no, but after what you told me about the findings of this psychic fellow, I...I'm not so sure. You see, way back in the early days before the Eglington Castle fire in which all of the records relating to the origin of the Masonic lodge here in Kilwinning were destroyed, this area had been terrorised by a Phantom Archer—"

"Oh, for Christ's sake!" McGovern's words were slow and enunciated, his incredulity blatant. "*A Phantom Archer?* I've heard it all now." He looked to the police surgeon. "Can you believe this rubbish?"

"Well...all things considered, the internal injuries would appear to be relatively consistent with high impact arrow wounds. Saying that, I've never actually seen an arrow wound but I daresay the damage inflicted could well be similar to those observable within the body."

Morrow's reply wasn't quite what McGovern had hoped for. "This is stupid. Do you honestly expect me to believe that there's a ghost out there...and that it's firing arrows at people?"

"I hate to be a pedant, sir...but you don't fire arrows, you shoot them," corrected Thom.

"That's all very good, but I'm afraid I don't buy any of this nonsense," said McGovern dismissively.

"So what are we going to do apart from wait until the killer strikes again?" Morrow asked.

It was a question McGovern was incapable of answering.

* * * *

Four days later, McGovern got out of his car, noticing immediately the small crowd of reporters gathered on the steps of the police station. Normally the press only descended when there was news of a murder, but this lot were clearly eager for any updates. With an angry shake of his head, he briefly contemplated whether he should respond to any of the forthcoming questions they would no doubt hurl his way or whether he should remain tight-lipped. Hands thrust into the pockets of his raincoat, he stalked forward, a scowl on his face.

"Has there been any further developments, inspector?"

"Is there any truth in the rumour that the killer's a woman?"

"Have you established a link yet between the victims?"

Ignoring the barrage of questions, McGovern pushed his way past, closing the main door behind him. Instantly, his eyes fell on the psychic who was absently looking at a poster on the wall. The man looked even more dishevelled than he had at their previous meeting. He walked over. "What do you want?" he asked truculently.

Lowry tried to smile, a mere thinning of his lips. It was clearly something he rarely did. "To help you," he replied. The leather jacket he wore was torn in places and his jeans were ripped at one knee. There was a haggard look to his lined face and his eyes were bloodshot. He obviously cared little for personal hygiene.

McGovern paused for a moment, thinking things over. "All right." He started towards his office, gesturing to the sordid psychic to follow, aware of the strong reek of stale body odour the man exuded. Once inside, he gestured to the other to take a seat before closing the door. He then sat down.

"After my discovery the other day, I started doing some research of my own." Scratching at a cluster of sores on his long chin, Lowry fixed McGovern with a steady stare. "I know you probably won't believe me, but I think I know the identity of the murderer."

"Don't tell me, it wouldn't by chance be a Sixteenth Century ghost, would it?" McGovern asked levelly.

"I take it then that you know about the Phantom Archer of Kilwinning?"

"I've heard something of the legend."

"It's no legend, inspector. It's historical fact. There has been a malign presence here in Kilwinning for well over a thousand years. When the founder of the town, Saint Winning, arrived here in the mid-Eighth Century he was forced to perform an exorcism in order to drive off a demonic power. This is recorded in the old chronicles. He was only partially successful. For four hundred years later, when work on the Abbey building began, there were numerous sightings of a dark spectre within the grounds. Many stonemasons died mysteriously and there was a prolonged hiatus in the construction with many believing the place to be cursed. A similar thing took place in the mid-Sixteenth Century only this time the records are slightly less ambiguous, and we have an exact number of the fatalities recorded. Twenty-seven deaths! The physicians of the day could offer no explanation. It's even recorded that the fire at Eglington Castle in 1544 may have been due to this wraith. And now, just over four hundred years later, this entity has returned and is once again embarking on its murderous campaign."

"So it would appear," retorted McGovern sarcastically.

"From your cynicism, it's pretty obvious that you don't believe a word of what I'm telling you."

"Well, try and see things from my position, Mr. Lowry. I admit that you've managed to baffle my police surgeon with your 'ability' of seeing injuries which aren't visible to the naked eye, but it'll take a lot more to convince me that some sort of vengeful spook is prowling around the town killing people. Now, if you've got nothing more to—"

The office door was flung wide by a ruddy-faced sergeant. "Sir, we've found another victim."

McGovern uttered a harsh oath. He got quickly to his feet.

"I'd like to accompany you, inspector. Like I said on our first meeting, I may be able to detect something vital from a more recent corpse than Mr. Buchanan's." Lowry stood up.

"No. That's completely out of the question." McGovern began forcibly ushering the psychic out. He grabbed his coat from where it hung on the back of the door.

"You're making a mistake. Just let me assist you. Knowing what you're up against, you're going to need my help."

"Get out of my way before I have you arrested," McGovern threatened.

Lowry decided to take a risk; to turn the tables. "You're being a fool. So much so that if you don't take me with you, I'll be sure to tell everyone of my involvement. I know it won't go down too well with—"

"You swine. Don't you try to blackmail me." McGovern briefly thought things over. The other was so damned adamant that he could help—to the extent that he was prepared to offer him an ultimatum. Despite the fact that he held the psychic in disdain, he decided to acquiesce. If Lowry were to prove obstructive, then he would personally make life very difficult for him. "Very well then, come along."

* * * *

The police had cordoned off the area by the time McGovern and Lowry turned up at the scene. The location was only a mile and a half from the police station—a veritable warren of residential, graffiti-covered and litter-strewn alleyways and backstreets. Despite the overall level of depressing decrepitude about the place all of the surrounding houses were fairly modern, certainly post-war; uniform, drab, grey buildings for the main.

After being guided through this squalid, built-up labyrinth by one of his constables, McGovern was led to where a sheet-covered hump lay on the cobbled ground.

Morrow emerged from someone's back gate. He nodded to the inspector but was quite surprised to see Lowry. "Welcome to Dodge City. Anyway, here's victim number seven. Mr. Tony Grimley. I've just been talking to a neighbour, and it would appear he heard screams in the night. He chose not to get involved. Apparently, there has been quite a bit of rowdiness and antisocial behaviour in this area." He crouched down. "Anyway, from a quick examination, the corpse is quite similar to the others with no visible evidence of wounding." He pulled back the covering.

Suddenly Lowry's cheeks swelled. With a sideways lurch, he reached out for a wall in order to support himself before vomiting. What he alone could see was ghastly. The dead man had been peppered with black-fletched arrows tipped with broadheads; bladed points designed specifically for killing. After a few further retches, he steadied himself, taking deep breaths. He had to pull himself together. Through glazed and disbelieving eyes, he could see that at least a dozen protruded from the corpse. One arrow had entered the unfortunate's mouth, no doubt during mid-scream, and had exited the back of his skull. Another arrow had pinned one of his hands to his chest. And yet, despite the multiple injuries, there was no trace whatsoever of any blood. There was, however, a strong look of absolute horror in the man's wide, staring eyes.

"Well?" McGovern asked. "What can you tell us?"

"I...take it you can't see the arrows..." Fighting back his revulsion, Lowry crouched down and grasped the available hand. He closed his eyes and began his unearthly, glossolalic mumbling.

Perplexed, McGovern stood staring, trying to envisage the victim as the psychic claimed to see him. Was any of this possible? He was a man who lived his life and based his career on the purely observable and detectable. Up until meeting Lowry, he had never experienced anything that even bordered on the supernatural. Now everything he had ever believed was being severely challenged.

Abruptly, Lowry's strange mutterings ended. He was breathing heavily, panting almost like an exhausted dog.

"Is he all right?" McGovern asked the police surgeon.

Violently, the psychic's head jerked back as though pulled by invisible ropes. His eyes sprang open—white and lifeless!

"Christ!" McGovern exclaimed. Instinctively, he pulled back. "What the hell's the matter with him?"

"I...I've no idea," voiced Morrow, uncertainly.

And then words started to spill from the psychic's mouth in a voice that was not his own. "Stabbing, freezing pain...in the leg. Like being skewered by an icicle. Fell to the ground. Sounds of...things whistling past. Managed to crawl. Terrible, cold pain in the chest. Again and again and again." Lowry was shaking violently yet still he maintained his grip on the corpse. "I see him. He's coming nearer. Dark, cowled shadow. Help me! He has no face! No face! Just a skull!" Suddenly he was thrown free. His eyes had returned to normal.

"What was all that about?" McGovern asked.

Lowry gulped. He scrambled to his feet and stood staring down at the corpse for a moment, trying to regain his composure. "I've never experienced anything like that before." He turned to face the two policemen. "I saw it! I saw everything! And it was horrific."

"So, what did you see?" McGovern was still having trouble accepting any of this.

"It was almost as though I was there. Not as a witness, but... as *him*." Lowry pointed to the dead man. He was trembling visibly. "This monster that is running amok takes the guise of a skeletal monk. It was armed with a bow with which it shoots its victims; an undead archer whose only purpose is to wreak unholy destruction. It cares not for whom it kills."

McGovern tapped Morrow on the shoulder and took him to one side. "Well? What's your take on this?"

"I really don't know." The police surgeon shook his head. "There's something bloody weird going on, that's for certain."

"Aye, *but a ghost?*" A deep frown creased McGovern's face. "Come on."

"I'm telling you, Andy. If there was any plausible alternative, I'd—" Morrow paused, noticing Sergeant Thom striding purposefully towards them.

McGovern turned.

"Sir, I've got some fresh information that I thought you might like to hear," said Thom excitedly.

"Let's hear it then."

"Well, it's concerning the..." Thom hesitated for a moment, "... ghost. You remember the story I told you about the Phantom Archer? With the assistance of the archivist of the Archery Society, I've discovered some mighty weird facts."

McGovern raised a hand, signalling to the other for silence. "Sergeant. I think we've all heard enough of this nonsense. May I remind you that—"

"I seriously think we should at least hear what he's got to say," Morrow interrupted. He for one was keen to find out whatever the other had to tell.

"All right, let's hear it." With some level of resignation, McGovern gestured to the sergeant to continue his tale, aware that the psychic had now ambled to within earshot. No doubt whatever fantastical account Thom was about to relate would serve only to embellish Lowry's wild speculations.

"Do you want to hear this here or back at the station?" Thom asked.

"Here's as good as anywhere. Hurry it up and let's get it over with."

"Very good, sir." Thom straightened. He removed a notebook from a pocket, consulted it briefly and then began. "The Society of Kilwinning Archers, like the Masonic Lodge, can trace its origins back to a remote period in history. Indeed, both can lay claim to being the oldest in Britain. Why, even the Barons of Roslin assembled their Grand Lodges at Kilwinning, and the Masonic Courts were held here. According to the annals of the Society it was first established by the Masons not to provide the inhabitants of Kilwinning with a leisurely pursuit but to better equip and train those with aptitude in combating what is referred to as 'Ye Terror of Ye Mother Ludge'. Now, the Mother Lodge, as you no doubt know, is of course the Masonic Lodge Number Zero. The 'Terror' is later referred to as 'The Phantom or Demon Archer'."

"There. What did I tell you?" remarked Lowry.

McGovern threw the psychic a black look before returning to face Thom. "So, assuming that this *thing* exists and it's out there right now—how exactly do we stop it? Do we call in a priest to excommunicate it or something?"

"Exorcise it," Lowry corrected.

"Not according to the accounts I read," began Thom. "As I said, the Society was set up with the explicit purpose of training archers, in the knowledge that only arrows dipped in the sacred well of St. Winning would destroy, or rather, banish this thing. I don't know whether it can be permanently slain."

"What rubbish." With a derisive snort, McGovern thrust his hands into his coat pockets and, shoulders hunched, began stalking back to his car, his mind a turmoil of riotous thoughts and emotions. To his way of thinking, he was the only sane one remaining.

* * * *

That evening there was a meeting at the Masonic Lodge during which McGovern had enquired whether any of the Brethren had heard anything concerning the legend of the Phantom Archer. Although he had initially expected his questions to be met with ridicule, he was somewhat surprised when certain aspects of Thom's account had been verified. One elderly Mason, a white-haired octogenarian who was known only as Brother 'Mac', had informed him that he himself was of the firm belief that the current spate of peculiar deaths was attributable to the very same spectre.

Returning home at half-past eleven, McGovern got out of his car and walked up the path to his front door. He was about to reach into a pocket for the key when suddenly he heard his phone ringing. With a growing sense of urgency, he unlocked the door and dashed along the hall, flicking on the light switch. He picked up the phone.

"Inspector?"

"Yes." He recognised the voice. "Is that you, Thom?"

"Aye. Sorry to have to bother you at this hour, sir, but we've got another body."

"Christ!" McGovern sighed deeply. Was there no end to this? Two deaths in as many days. Things were getting out of hand. "Any details?" he asked.

"It's...Lowry. Your psychic friend. He was found in the Abbey grounds not twenty minutes ago. It appears he'd weny out to try and hunt this thing down."

"What do you mean by that?"

"Well, he was armed with a longbow—one that we believe had been stolen from the supply kept at the Archery Society club hut. He had a quiver full of arrows. I don't doubt that he'd taken the liberty of dipping them in the waters of St. Winning's Well. Poor bastard must've thought that he could destroy this thing."

"Is his body still there and has Morrow been informed?"

"Yes...to both."

"Right. I'll meet you there in about—" McGovern consulted his wristwatch. "—fifteen minutes." He put the phone down. He was just about to go into his kitchen, to get himself a quick snack, when a loud series of raps on his front door caused him to jump. He started back along the hallway. "Hold on. I'm coming." Upon opening the door, he was somewhat surprised to see Brother 'Mac' stood on the doorstep, a bundle of books under one arm.

"I thought you might find some of these of interest," said the old man, handing the books over. "There's a few that relate to the origins of the town. And one or two that tell you more about the legend of the Phantom Archer. By all means, feel free to hang onto them for as long as you need."

McGovern hesitated a moment, puzzled. "Oh...thanks." He hadn't expected this. He looked down at the topmost book. It was titled *Supernatural Scotland*. The one below read *Ghosts of Ye Olde Kilwynning*.

"That's all right, Brother. Happy reading." Without a further word, 'Mac' turned and started down the garden path.

* * * *

A chill drizzle fell from the midnight sky as, in his constable's torchlight, McGovern stared down at Lowry's crumpled body. The unfortunate lay on the hard ground less than fifteen feet from one of the Abbey's ruined walls. It was hard to tell from the obviously pained rictus frozen on his face whether he had died from acute agony or abject terror, although the inspector believed it was probably both. In spite of his best efforts, he could not help but imagine the psychic's corpse bristling like an obscene voodoo doll, transfixed not with pins, but with arrows.

A longbow lay nearby close to a scattering of arrows and a leather quiver, the carrying strap having come loose.

"I don't know about you, Andy, but the more I see things like this the more I'm coming round to believing in this Phantom Archer." Fearfully, Morrow began looking around him. The three of them were now standing in a small pool of radiance in a seemingly nebulous void of clinging shadows. The looming dark ruins of the Abbey with its large tower were but tenebrous black outlines—providing countless places for unnameable and unholy things to lurk. Maybe even now they were being watched and scrutinised with malign intent. Maybe even now some terror from beyond death was lining them up as its next victim.

"Who found him?" asked McGovern.

"He was found by a Mr. David McGuiness, one of the Masons from the lodge who was returning home. Apparently, he always comes this way to avoid the drunks who gather outside the Cross

Keys," said Thom reflectively. "It would seem that our warning for folk to stay indoors at night has largely gone unheeded."

McGovern nodded. He had talked to Brother McGuiness earlier that night. He crouched down, considering for one moment what he would have done had he the deceased's alleged power to detect ethereal wounds. Had this man died from being struck repeatedly by ghostly arrows? There was clearly no denying the fact that the other had firmly believed in the fiendish bowman.

An owl hooted somewhere out there in the darkness.

"I don't know about either of you two, but I feel uncomfortable about being here," Thom admitted. Shivering, he stared wildly around. "It's almost as though we're being watched. The sooner the meat-wagon arrives to collect our friend here so that we can go the better."

McGovern shared his constable's sentiments although he was loath to come out and say it.

"The ambulance will be here soon," said Morrow. Noticing approaching headlights over by the entrance to the Abbey grounds he turned to the inspector. "In fact, here they are now. I'll get some photographs of the corpse in situ and then I'll accompany him to the morgue." He sighed heavily. "Looks like it's going to be another long night."

"For me as well," muttered McGovern.

"Why's that—are you coming along with me?" asked Morrow.

"No. It's just that a friend dropped off a load of books and I think it's probably about time that I started to give this Phantom Archer theory a bit more credence. Not that I'm expecting to find anything of use, but you never know."

* * * *

"Can you get your hands on a spare bow?" McGovern gulped down his sixth black coffee of the morning, crumpled the plastic cup in his fist and tossed it angrily into a waste bin. Despite the fact that he had reached some level of resignation regarding just what had to be done, he was in a foul mood. He had spent most of the morning reading, trawling through the supernatural literature he had been provided with and consequently, he had had little sleep. In addition, there had been a particularly obstreperous clamouring crowd of reporters which he had been forced to deal with at the station gates. A crowd that had somehow gotten wind that there had been another unexplained death.

"A bow? You mean a longbow?" asked Thom.

"Yes. I take it you can get one for me. You're also going to have to give me a crash course in how to use one. I did a bit of target archery many years ago just after I left school, but I—"

"So, I take it that you now believe that the Phantom Archer is real, sir?"

"I don't know what to believe." McGovern shook his head. "However, I read some rather interesting things that, let's just say, have challenged my earlier scepticism. If what I read is true, then that poor bastard Lowry didn't stand a chance."

"Oh, what makes you say that? Surely, he had the right weapon for the job, and I wouldn't be at all surprised if the arrows he had with him had been dipped in St. Winning's Well, like it says in the legend."

"Be that as it may, he was lacking certain..." McGovern cast his mind back to what it had mentioned in the book he had consulted, "...periaptic items. Articles of clothing that would have offered him protection."

Thom raised a curious eyebrow. "What like—a helmet and a suit of plate mail armour?"

"No, believe it or not, *this*." Reaching down, McGovern retrieved a black briefcase, which he placed on his desk. He clicked it open, reached in and withdrew a Master Mason's apron, a green collar and sash, a pair of white gloves and a collection of medals. "According to the legend, the Phantom Archer can only be vanquished by a Brother of the Mystic Tie—a Freemason."

* * * *

Darkness had fallen and everything was unnaturally still and quiet, as cold and silent as the grave. McGovern, resplendent in his attire, if not a trifle unusual in appearance, garbed as he was in his Masonic regalia and clutching a longbow, stood for a moment at the end of the long, misty alleyway and peered along it, holding his breath, listening intently as though expecting to hear the sound of stealthy footsteps creeping up at his back. Then, when he could bear the tension no longer, he snapped his head round and glanced apprehensively behind him. But there was nothing there; only the empty blackness, mocking him silently.

And yet he had the feeling that there was *something* out there. Something that he couldn't see but could sense quite easily sent his nerves tingling and crawling, lifting the small hairs on the back of his neck like hackles on a frightened dog. He knew he should have brought someone out with him, but he knew that would only be putting them under incredible danger. He had ruminated on whether he should have tried to recruit some of the Brethren to assist him in driving out this evil but had finally decided that it was his duty, both as a policeman and a Mason, to do this alone.

Fear came creeping out of the black shadows at him, encircling him, surging over him like a dark, raging tide. With an effort, he suppressed a shiver of nervous tension that shuddered through his body. If only he could thrust away the dark, nagging thoughts that were in the innermost corners of his mind, push them away, so that they might be completely forgotten. This, however, was where too much knowledge proved deleterious. For, having learnt about the Phantom Archer his mind had become a veritable seething witch's cauldron filled with folkloric night terrors. He had found himself reflecting that this was the trouble when one came to investigate anything like this. Rumours were vague and nebulous things, which had been twisted and distorted out of all recognition during the intervening centuries and seeking the grain of truth that lay at the bottom of all things, was like looking for the needle in the proverbial haystack. And yet, once one opened one's mind to the possibility that such things existed, it set in motion a much darker spiral—at its end, death or incurable insanity.

With a mental effort, he pulled himself together, drew in a deep breath and stalked forward slowly. For an instant, he thought he heard a weird, chuckling laugh at his shoulder, but with an effort he refrained from looking around, certain that it must've been nothing more than his overwrought imagination playing tricks on him. He felt his mind beginning to waver again as a tiny shaking tremor in his legs set in. If only he could push away the idea that there was something in the dark; a half-seen thing lurking somewhere in the shadows around him, he would feel a little better. But try as he would, he could not exorcise the things on his mind; awful things that bunched the muscles of his stomach, tightened them into hard knots of fear, sending his heart racing in an uneven rhythm in his chest.

A light chill drizzle began to fall from the dark skies.

With a nervous gulp, he looked over his shoulder. Gripping the longbow, a sanctified arrow nocked and ready to be shot, he turned and stared down the alley again, trying to throw his sight into the shadows. For a good two minutes he stood motionless, contemplating, well aware that it was in places such as this that the thing he had come to hunt down—if indeed it existed—was known to strike its victims. Countless people no doubt used this alleyway, but that was in the hours of daylight, when the terrors of the night were banished and easily forgotten, relegated to things of superstition and nightmare.

There was no way he was going to be able to continue his task if he could not overcome his inner fears. He might as well have stayed at home. Mustering his courage, he entered the dingy tunnel of darkness, eyes focused on the streetlights at the far end. With each step he felt as though he was entering a hellish domain; fearing at any moment that some eldritch shadow, some cowled monstrosity, would detach itself from the alley walls behind him and shoot a spectral arrow into his back. That others would follow, trailing an icy, ethereal, blue-green mist in their wake.

His heart was thumping loudly in his chest. Blood pounded at his temples. Almost mechanically, he picked up his brisk pace, his walk now becoming a stride, eager to exit the alley and reach the relative light and sanity of the street now becoming more visible before him.

At the mid-way point, he could feel his nerves begin to falter. This was where he was most vulnerable, the lights at either end, weakest. It was here that the foul things lurked and where they were at their strongest. Not for the first time that evening did the sheer absurdity of what he was doing—or hoping to do—strike him. Was he insane? For here he was prowling around the empty, dead streets in search of a killer that, if the damned legend was true, wasn't even remotely human.

With a hiss, a startled cat leapt from his path, half-scaring the life from him. His stride became a jog and then a sprint. In his mind, he saw the remaining forty yards or so of shrouded darkness elongate, the distance stretched as though reflected in a funhouse mirror. And there was something in that reflection. Half-seen, tenebrous images and suggestions of hideous, ghastly, tentacled figures in front and behind him. Things that oozed and dripped and slithered. Things that defied the realm of normality and classification. Things that sought to bar his way or drag him back kicking and screaming.

Suddenly, the horrifying phantasmagoria vanished, melted away. He had reached the other end. Emerging from the darkness, McGovern took a few deep breaths. He found himself on a slightly rundown residential street. There were no lights on in any of the houses nor were there any passing cars or fellow pedestrians.

Far-off, dull-sounding church bells began to toll, striking midnight, the sound eerily amplified in the chill night air. Within five minutes he was at one end of the High Street and heading for the ruined Abbey.

Lazy, dense clouds drifted away, permitting the bright moonlight to drench the ancient ruins, brightening them in an almost unholy, eldritch effulgence. The crumbling walls and arches of the decaying cloisters and outlying structures that formed the nave and the transept glistened eerily as though dripping fungal growths of hideous shape.

Shoes crunching on the gravel path which lay underneath, McGovern gave a deep breath and headed inside, edging into the interior, the dark, and looming shadow of the Abbey tower on his right. It was here that the Society of Kilwinning Archers held their annual papingo shoot—a rather archaic archery discipline that involved shooting vertically up the face of the tower in an attempt to hit a small target placed on a pole which projected from it some hundred and ten feet up.

McGovern wondered briefly if his target was going to be any easier to strike. With that thought in mind, he stopped, straining his senses, trying to pick out any unusual nocturnal noises. There was nothing. It was as though a black blanket of silence had descended, smothering everything. Yet it seemed as though there was movement at the edge of his vision; hideous, evil things had vanished abruptly or crouched still whenever he turned his head to look directly at them. A paralysing fear struck him, rooting him to the spot.

There was a sudden, diabolical moan from near the entrance to the cemetery as a cowled horror detached itself from a pool of darkness, gliding unnaturally out of the shadows. Two points of lambent red light appeared on a level with where the eyes would be.

McGovern's nerve faltered. Desperately, he tried to drag his gaze from those hellish points of light but found it impossible to do so. It was nearing, moving effortlessly over the uneven ground, floating towards him, rising over portions of tumbled wall.

For an instant, he saw a greenish blur and then a whistling projectile shot past his head, breaking the terrible hold the spectre had on him. The thing uttered a dreadful banshee's wail, lamenting over the fact that it had missed. With unearthly speed it launched a second arrow, this one speeding straight and true for McGovern's heart. He cried out as, at the last moment, it was deflected by something invisible, disappearing into the darkness, a comet-like trail of bilious yellow vapour in its wake. One of the Masonic jewels fell from his black suit, and lay warped and melting on the ground, its talismanic powers spent.

Mustering his courage, he raised his own longbow and released the nocked arrow, cursing in frustration as his weak attempt missed by a considerable distance. He had four arrows remaining in the quiver he wore at his hip. Dashing for cover, he heard another arrow snap sharply off a wall nearby.

His common sense was screaming at him to flee from this place. To get away while he still could. There was nothing but death and madness here. He ran for an archway, his knuckles white where he gripped the bow. Leaping through it, he then sprang to his right, his back to the coarse brickwork, his heart thumping. A cold, clammy sweat trickled down his face.

Believing that the wraith was behind him, McGovern threw a quick glance over his shoulder, through the archway. He could see nothing. He waited for a moment, imagining briefly that this was no doubt similar to the shoot-outs some of his associates in the police had been involved in—living with the uncertainty over whether your next move would be your last. However, this was worse, much worse.

Only the faith he had in the protective powers of the regalia he wore kept him from running headlong into the darkness. Cautiously, he began to edge back, eyes alert, ready to for any sudden movements. And then he saw the ghastly being rise above the stone opening, landing atop it. Before he could act, the thing had launched an arrow. It sped unerringly towards him before shattering into fragments off some protective barrier before him.

Although unhurt, the force of the strike knocked McGovern back. He lost his footing, collided with an ancient upthrusting headstone and slumped to the ground.

The phantom drifted down from its vantage point. It drew its bow back and shot again.

Sparks flew before McGovern's eyes as the ghostly missile, its point barbed and cruel, glanced against that mystical shield. Was it just his imagination or had he seen something almost like a glass barrier before his eyes? If so then it was beginning to crack and he knew that his defences wouldn't remain in place for long, certainly not against this continuous battering. A further arrow struck home—this one lodging into the protective screen, the vicious point mere inches from his chest.

Desperately, he scrambled to his feet. Drawing an arrow from his quiver, he nocked it, drew back the bowstring with all his strength, willing his anger into the pull, and—with an ear-splitting bang, the longbow splintered along the lines of its laminations, leaving him with nothing more effective than a stick.

A bloodcurdling cry of triumph screeched forth as the Phantom Archer moved in for the kill. It was now less than ten feet way, hovering just above the ground. Its eyes were twin fiery points of pure evil. At point-blank range, it drew back, preparing to launch an arrow from its seemingly unending supply.

The arrow smote into the barrier. McGovern felt it strike his chest. The pain was instantaneous. Freezing. It was the touch of death. Yet as he had discovered from his dealings with the victims of this horror, it appeared that more than one arrow was required to kill. Gritting his teeth, he snatched the three remaining shafts in his hand and, with a cry of rage, lunged forward, plunging them directly into the cowled terror. The legend regarding this thing's destruction had said nothing about using a bow and he just had to hope that this far cruder method would prove as effective.

The ghost's head flew back as it wailed its agony to the dark, uncaring skies. Its bow fell from a skeletal hand.

"You bastard!" McGovern drove the arrows in deeper, withdrew them and stabbed again and again.

The Phantom Archer retreated, its movements now far less fluid—an indication that it was severely injured. It began to dissolve. Disrupted, the age-old demon that had terrorised Kilwinning down the centuries was lit in a haze of sparking, violet-green energy. The black cowl melted away, revealing the dreadful skeletal corpse beneath. Portions of bone began to implode, the bulk of the spectre's incorporeal self simply disintegrating, the composite particles suspended in air and then gone. The revenant that had evolved from the ancient demon that St. Winning had only partially banished over a millennium ago vanished.

Still gripping the three arrows, McGovern realised he was breathing heavily, unsure whether it was gone for good.

With a sudden dark flash which lit the area in a twenty-foot radius in a spectral glow, the Phantom Archer tore its way back from whatever dimension it had temporarily been vanquished to. Wailing like a tortured cat, it reached out with a skeletal hand from whatever hell had tried to claim it, struggling to break free into this world once more.

Snatching up the undead being's bow, McGovern dropped two arrows and shot the third straight into it. Then, his damage done, he watched in stunned disbelief as the unearthly entity was drawn back once more into the nebulous void, the swirling vortex of darkness from which it had emerged. The void was compressed to a single glowing point. Then it blinked out of existence.

"I did it...by Christ, I did it!" mumbled McGovern, looking around and noting nothing out of the ordinary. It was only then that he felt a weird tingling in his right hand where he still grasped the wraith's bow. Alarmed, he saw a web-like tracery of dark veins appear just under the skin. A rivulet of black fluid pulsed out of his hand along the arteries at his wrist almost as though *it* were the heart.

With that, he knew he was now doomed—a slave to the bow. Deeds of evil were promised and revealed and, with the weapon that had now formed a wicked, parasitic bond with him, he would become a new agent of chaos and death.

Smiling evilly, he set off, assured in the knowledge that the unwary always made tempting targets and that, to an archer, the best way to a person's heart was always through their ribcage.

Two

The Gory Bells

It had rained more or less consistently for two weeks and in addition to localised flooding, a nauseating mist had risen from the Clyde, obscuring and polluting much of Glasgow. The districts south of the river were the hardest hit and the health authority advised people to stay indoors if possible and to avoid drinking un-boiled water, fearing it may have become contaminated with raw sewage. In addition, there were the rats—huge, vicious creatures that now swarmed freely in abandoned buildings and amidst the heaps of overflowing rubbish which clogged numerous alleys.

It was widely rumoured that at least one unfortunate had fallen victim to the ravenous rodents.

John McAlpine heard the squeaking and the rustling as he made his way to *Dirty Betty's*—ranked as one of the roughest pubs in the Gorbals. He was a typical, heavy-drinking, overweight, dour, diabetic Glaswegian, who had not worked for over thirty-five years; unable to find meaningful employment after the collapse of the shipbuilding industry. Not one for heeding medical recommendations, he also smoked like a chimney, despite having suffered three heart attacks and having been pronounced clinically dead on two separate occasions. Indeed, it was a miracle that he was still alive; a fact often cursed by his long-suffering wife, Marjorie.

"That them bloody rats, again?" Marjorie—a small, white-haired woman with a terribly wrinkled face—drew her raincoat tighter. She peered, myopically, into the gloom through her thick-lensed glasses. "It's aboot time the council did summat. Christ! Ye'd think they'd forgotten aboot us."

"They probably have. Bastards!" Hands in pockets, McAlpine trudged on. The rain was getting heavy, and he was in desperate need of a drink. In the distance, he could hear a chorus of angry, drunken shouts.

"Elsie doon the stairs said that all the schools have had tae shut because o' this fog. Folk are scared tae send their weans oot. It's terrible, if ye ask me."

McAlpine lit a cigarette and flicked away the spent match. "Pure shite, that's what it is. Christ, they even had tae cancel the Celtic-Rangers game."

"Aye, so I heard. Anyway, do ye think 'One-Armed Bob' will be in tonight?"

'One-Armed Bob' was a relative newcomer to *Dirty Betty's* and, despite his advanced years, he had become something of a hit with a few of the female clientele. His name was not derived from the fact that he was missing a limb but rather from his addiction to playing the old-fashioned one-armed bandit slot machine in one of the pub's side-rooms.

"So ye fancy him, dae ye?"

"Well, he's a bit old for me but at least he's a gentleman. He always buys me an' Agnes a drink. Talkin' o' Agnes, did ye hear what happened tae her Wullie?"

"No."

"He got hit by a bus in Motherwell."

"What was he daein' there?" McAlpine asked gruffly.

"Visitin' his mother, accordin' tae Agnes."

"Christ, is she still goin'? She must be comin' up on ninety." With a clumsy step, McAlpine stood on a particularly unpleasant dog turd.

"*Gads!*" Marjorie muttered, wafting the foul stench from her nostrils.

Uttering a string of expletives, McAlpine used the pavement kerb to scrape away the worst of the excrement. By the time he had finished, the fog had thickened, reducing visibility to ten feet or so. Crossing a cobbled street, he and his wife turned left down a narrow alley. At the far end, its lights barely shining through the gloom, was *Dirty Betty's*.

* * * *

Only a handful of drinkers were inside the pub and, apart from a tall man who disappeared into the squalid, urinous toilets when McAlpine and his wife entered, they were all regulars.

"All right, John? Ye're in luck the night, ye fat bastard," Jimmy Dixon cried out by way of greeting. The scrawny, heavily whiskered, runt of a man rose from his chair, empty pint glass in hand, and smiled at Marjorie. "All right, hen?"

"No' so bad, Jimmy. How're ye keepin'?" Marjorie asked. She took off her raincoat and hung it on a peg.

Dixon shrugged his thin shoulders. "Ach, good days, bad days."

"What dae ye mean, I'm in luck the night?" McAlpine asked, a modicum of aggression in his tone. He spotted several more of his cronies sat at their usual table in the corner.

"I mean, ye don't have tae buy any drinks," Dixon answered.

Shug, the landlord, started pouring a pint. "Aye, that's right. So, usual, John?"

"What is this, Christmas?" McAlpine was pleasantly surprised. He took his drink and knocked back a hefty swallow.

"No. It's better than that." Dixon nodded towards the toilets. "See that guy who's just nipped intae the bogs?"

"What aboot him?" McAlpine wiped ale froth from his lips.

"He's a Cambridge professor an' he's put a hundred pounds behind the bar," Shug answered. "He says he's after information on weird happenin's in the area."

"*Weird happenin's?* Christ! There's always weird happenin's goin' on around here," quipped Marjorie, taking her double whisky from the landlord.

"Cambridge professor, ma arse!" McAlpine snorted. "What would a Cambridge professor be daein' in here?"

"I told ye. He's wantin' tae know aboot weird things," Shug answered.

McAlpine cocked a suspicious eye towards the toilets. "What dae ye mean? What sort o' weird things?"

"Things that go bump in the night." Dixon screwed up his face in order to make himself look scary. He was about to say something else, when the toilet door opened and the man in question emerged.

With barely a nod to the newcomers, the stranger went back to the table where McAlpine's other cronies were waiting.

"I'll introduce ye," said Dixon.

Drink in hand, McAlpine nodded. *Dirty Betty's* had been his local for almost all of his adult life—the one place that offered some kind of solace from the day-to-day drudgery of his impoverished and mundane existence. Over the course of that time, he had witnessed the grim reality of life in the Gorbals; where social decay, lack of employment, community housing, poor education, drug use, gang warfare and sectarianism were rife. He had seen countless brawls, several stabbings and two shootings—all committed in the very room he was in and yet not once had he encountered anyone quite like Professor Rupert Reed; the mystery man who had paid upfront for information.

"Hey, mister." Dixon looked slightly embarrassed. "This is ma good pal, Big John."

"Pleased to meet you, John." Reed spoke with a cultured, non-Scottish accent. He removed a notebook and pen from an inner jacket pocket. "I trust you got yourself a drink?"

"Aye, cheers." McAlpine sat himself down next to Billy Lamby and Tam Hannah, men he had known for over thirty years. Briefly, he appraised Reed, noting the smart and stylish suit, expensive-looking overcoat and the gold watch the man wore. He had dark hair, turning grey at the temples and deep brown, smouldering eyes which for some unexplainable reason unsettled the Glaswegian. In terms of age, he reckoned the stranger to be several years older than himself, perhaps late sixties.

Dixon and Marjorie took their seats round the table.

"Ye were sayin' that ye're interested in hearin' aboot strange things that have happened around here, is that right?" asked Lamby. He was even fatter than McAlpine and was often mistaken for Hamish Imlach, the renowned Scottish folk singer, of whom he was known to occasionally impersonate.

"That's correct," Reed replied.

McAlpine lit a cigarette, well aware that Shug had long turned a blind eye to the ban on smoking on the premises. "What exactly is it ye want tae know?" He was becoming increasingly suspicious, wondering just who this person was and the reason behind his interest. As someone who lived on the fringe of legality, he was hesitant about divulging anything to someone he knew nothing about. Reed could be a police detective, sounding them all out or worse—an official from the benefits department.

"Aye, I mean, it's all well an' good o' ye tae come in here an' sweeten us up wi' drinks but just what is it ye're really after?" asked Marjorie, sharing her husband's wariness.

"I'm a researcher into...unsolved mysteries and paranormal events. I'm currently gathering information for a book I plan on writing about strange British urban legends." Reed took a sip from his glass of blackcurrant and lemonade.

"We've got problems enough round here without ye bringin' ghosts an' ghoulies intae it," Hannah said, his tone surly and argumentative. "There's nae work; there's nae decent hooses, the weans are all starvin', the streets are filled wi' numpties an' druggies who'd stab ye as soon as look at ye, all for a few bob, an' we've now got rats the size o' dogs roamin' all o'er the place. And here ye are, ye southern bastard, askin' us for—"

"Steady on, Tam," Dixon interrupted. "Fair's fair. The man's got us in some drinks so the least we can dae is be civil an' help him oot."

"You will be generously reimbursed for your assistance," Reed smiled.

McAlpine liked the sound of that. Tapping ash from his cigarette into an ashtray, he found himself respecting the stranger's nerve. Only the diehard drunks or the mentally unstable would come into this part of Glasgow, never mind *Dirty Betty's*, talking sophisticated as he did and making it known that he had money about his person.

Now that there were no other customers in the pub, Shug came over and joined them, drawing up a chair next to Marjorie. He too had heard the words 'generously reimbursed'. "I once saw summat that might interest ye."

"Don't ye start," Hannah warned, wagging a finger at the barman. "There's nothin' weird goin' on. Nothin'! All this talk o' ghosts an' things—it's all rubbish. Utter crap." Like most of the denizens of *Dirty Betty's*, the more he drank, the more belligerent he became. There was little doubt that he was the worst of the group, his notoriety as a troublemaker and drunkard well earned. It was claimed that he would argue with his own shadow if there was no one else present and the fact that he had been drinking since late morning did not bode well for a peaceful evening.

"Aye, so ye say, Tam, but how do ye explain that Daddy Longlegs carry on we had here aboot ten years ago?" said Dixon.

"Ah, the Daddy Longlegs mystery." Reed crossed his arms. "That was indeed most interesting…and, to this day, unexplained. Glasgow's equivalent of Spring-Heeled Jack."

McAlpine felt a tiny tremor of an old fear run through his body. The events in question had concerned the night-time exploits of a bizarrely dressed, nine-foot tall being with long, spindly legs and a horrendous, demonic face. At first, the reports had come from drunks returning home late at night, but there had also been several sightings by more credible witnesses, including a newspaper reporter and two police officers. For the best part of a year the creature had terrorised the Glasgow slums, creeping into bedrooms, peeking through windows and pouncing on the unwary. And whilst no deaths had been attributed to the frightening apparition, there was no denying the fact that many had lived in fear of encountering it.

"Hah! That was just some drugged-up heid-the-baw on stilts," commented Hannah, dismissively. "Nothin' scary aboot that."

"Well, what aboot the 'Scabby-Daggy' men?" said Shug. "That was a story ma grandfather used tae tell."

"What's that aboot?" Dixon asked.

"'The Scabby-Daggy' was the old name given to the Medieval lepers," Reed explained. "This part of Glasgow used to be a leper refuge. In fact, it's quite plausible that the etymology of the word 'Gorbals' is derived from 'gory bells'—the bells which the lepers and those who cared for them wore in order to warn others of their presence."

"Is that right? Christ! I've lived here all ma life, an' I didnae ken that," Dixon exclaimed in surprise. He turned to McAlpine. "But ye're bein' awfully quiet, John. What's the strangest or scariest thing ye've ever seen?"

McAlpine put his glass down on the heavily stained table. "The scariest thing I've ever seen?"

"I ken what it was," said Hannah. "It was that time the polis turned up at yer door wi' that repo man who was after yer telly."

McAlpine shook his head. A strangely thoughtful look had come over his unshaven, unpleasant face. "No. It wasnae that."

"Then I bet it was that time me an' ye got absolutely blootered an' went intae that Rangers pub o'er in Barrhead an' them mad bastards stormed in wi' chainsaws." It was something Lamby could joke about now but at the time it had been absolutely terrifying. Three people had been killed in the incident and they had barely managed to escape; desperately fleeing the scene, pursued by a bloodthirsty mob that wanted to carve them up and possibly eat them.

"No, no' that either." McAlpine stubbed out his cigarette. He looked across at Shug. "Can ye get me a double whisky? I'm goin' tae need it if I'm tae tell this story. For believe me, this'll chill ye tae the bone."

* * * *

The tale that McAlpine related was known, in part, to some gathered there. It concerned events that had taken place fifty years ago, when, on the twenty-third of September 1954, over two hundred youngsters had ran amok in the Southern Necropolis intent on killing a 'vampire' which had supposedly murdered and devoured two young boys.

"Yes, I remember reading about it," Reed revealed. "It was big news at the time, appearing in several newspapers. The 'vampire' in question was allegedly seven foot tall and was reported as having iron teeth."

McAlpine nodded. The cigarette he had clamped between his nicotine-stained fingers had nearly burnt out.

"I didnae ken ye were there," said Marjorie. "Ye've never told me anythin' aboot this."

"It was a long time ago, Marjorie. I was only a boy o' twelve or thirteen. Besides, things like that ye try tae forget." McAlpine knocked back the last of his whisky.

"I used tae ken a guy who was friends wi' one o' the teachers that was there at the time," added Lamby. "He told me that—"

"An escaped eejit from the nuthouse, no doubt wi' a set of braces, was scarin' the weans in the cemetery by pretendin' tae be Dracula," Hannah interrupted.

"Will ye shut up!?" McAlpine shouted.

"Aye, shut up, Tam, ye annoyin' bastard or I'll fling ye oot," Shug threatened.

Cursing under his breath and shaking his head, Hannah slumped back in his seat. He had been thrown out of *Dirty Betty's* numerous times and he knew that if such were to happen again it could be weeks before he would be allowed to return.

"This, Southern Necropolis…it's not that far from here?" inquired Reed.

"It's just up the road a bit," Dixon answered. "I live in the block o' flats next tae it. It's a hell o' a place. No' for the faint-hearted, if ye ken what I mean."

"I seem tae remember readin' summat aboot how all the weans from the nearby schools poured intae the cemetery armed wi' wooden stakes an' garlic an' all that kind o' stuff ye see in the old Hammer horror films," said Lamby. "Apparently news o' the 'vampire' spread like wildfire throughout the playgrounds an' it was that which got all the weans riled up."

"Was it no' summat tae dae wi' the comics they were readin'?" Marjorie queried.

"Yes, it's coming back to me," Reed admitted, stroking his chin. "Religious leaders, teachers and some politicians blamed the children's exploits on the new wave of lurid American comics, such as *Tales from the Crypt* and *Dark Mysteries*. Others put it down to a form of mass hysteria."

"I can tell ye, here an' now, that that's rubbish."

All eyes turned to McAlpine.

"Now, I've never spoken aboot this before, tae anybody, an' I don't really ken why I should be tellin' it tae ye lot the night. But…" McAlpine paused, his mind trying to harken back to that dark time half a century ago.

"Go on," Shug prompted.

"Dae any o' ye remember the 'Dummy'?" McAlpine asked, referring to one of the many down and outs who had eked out a pitiful existence, scrounging and scavenging on the derelict streets; one who had become something of a local character partly due to the fact that he was obviously an imbecile; unable to talk, his speech limited to a handful of guttural grunts.

"Oh, Christ aye," Lamby answered. "How could ye forget? He had more than one foot in the grave an' he stank tae the high heavens. Ye used tae see him a lot prowlin' around the Gallowgate."

"See that 'Dummy'! He gave me the creeps," Dixon admitted. "The way he'd just slouch aboot in that same old, big, dirty coat. I don't ken if any o' ye ever saw him up close, but Christ was he weird lookin'. Bulgin' eyes an' sunken cheeks; skin an' hair the colour o' chalk. A right freak!"

"Aye, but he wasnae born like that," McAlpine replied. "His real name was Alec Foster an' me an' him were the best o' pals at school where he was a right brainy bastard—top o' his class for every subject. Believe it or no' but he was also good lookin'—a hit wi' all the lassies. That said, he had a mean streak in him no doubt due tae him bein' abused by his drunken father. Anyhow, one day we were in the playground an' some guy I thought was a new teacher came up tae us sayin' that there was a monster in the graveyard an' did we want tae go an' have a look."

"Christ, ye weren't daft enough tae fall for that, were ye?" said Hannah.

"There was no way I was goin' tae go wi' him…but, Alec, well, he was intae all them stupid comics an' things that Marjorie mentioned an' he got all excited. I told him no' tae be so stupid but he'd made up his mind. When the dinner bell went, he sneaked oot through a hole in the fence. I remember standin' there, thinkin' tae maself what I should dae next. I thought aboot goin' tae get a teacher but maybe, deep down, I too was interested tae see this monster, so I decided tae go after him." A fresh pint had been put down in front of McAlpine and he took a large drink.

"What happened next?" asked Reed.

McAlpine put his drink down. "The guy who'd told us aboot the monster was nowhere tae be seen, however I caught up wi' Alec at the bottom o' Cumberland Street near tae where an old picture hoose used tae be. I tried tae talk some sense intae him but he wasnae havin' any o' it. It was as we were arguin' that two younger weans, Ralphie Tucker an' his wee brother, Pat, came runnin' towards us, yellin' an' screamin', sayin' that they'd seen a ghost in the graveyard, walkin' aboot in broad daylight. I freely admit that by this time I was beginnin' tae get a bit uneasy, but it just made Alec all the more determined tae go an' see it. I remember him givin' them a handful o' sweeties an' bullyin' the two brothers intae showin' us where it was. So off we went, Alec practically draggin' them along. The main gate was padlocked but we all knew a place where there was a tree ye could use tae climb o'er the wall. Ralphie was screamin' but Alec threatened tae—"

"Not wanting to interrupt but could I possibly get a drink?"

All eyes turned to the bar where 'One-Armed Bob' was stood, having entered *Dirty Betty's* unnoticed. He was a tall man in his early eighties, dignified, smartly-dressed and with a definite ex-military look to him. Indeed, in past conversations he had spoken fondly of his time as an officer in the *Black Watch*.

"I'm sorry," Shug apologised, rising from his chair. "We've been havin' a talk aboot a thing that happened in the past an'—"

'One-Armed Bob' raised a hand. "Don't worry. Now, a large rum, if you please."

"Be sure to take that from the money I put behind the bar," said Reed.

"Why, that's most kind of you." With a nod of appreciation, 'One-Armed Bob' took his drink and headed to the cubicle to indulge in his favourite pastime—feeding coins into the slot machine.

"I'm afraid the puggy's oot o' order," said Shug. "It'll no' be fixed until the morrow."

"So why don't ye come o'er an' sit wi' us?" Marjorie asked, seeing the disappointment on the elderly man's face. "Ye can sit next tae me."

McAlpine watched as the gambling-obsessed octogenarian sat down beside his wife. He then took another drink before continuing with his recollection. "So anyhow, there we were, now in the graveyard; me, Alec an' the two Tucker boys. Now, I don't ken if ye remember but there used tae be an old steelworks at the back o' it an' sometimes that'd pump oot this dreadful, shite-smellin', red smoke. Well, that day the place was full o' it. Dependin' on which way the wind was blowin', sometimes ye could hardly see a thing; except for the rows o' headstones an' the odd statue. The Tucker boys were greetin' their eyes oot but Alec wouldnae let them go until they'd shown him the monster. We went doon one o' the paths an' I remember it was deathly quiet. Then, all o' a sudden, there came this horrible wailin' noise. Well, that was it— broon trooser time."

"He means he keiched himself or should I say…dropped one in his underpants," Hannah elucidated for Reed's benefit, finishing his sentence by putting on a mock, upper-class English accent.

"An' so would ye have," McAlpine replied harshly. "Panic set in. I froze; unable tae move. For all his talk o' wantin' tae see the monster, Alec buggered off sharpish. Then, somethin'—a tall, black, hooded shadow—came runnin' oot o' the smoke; dirty, big, grey gnashers in its gob. It grabbed wee Pat Tucker an' when his brother went tae help, it went for him. The two o' them were screamin' at me tae save them but there was no way I was goin' tae fight that thing so I scarpered. It might've been just ma imagination but I'm sure I could hear horrible slurpin' an' gobblin' noises."

"Jeez-o! Ye wouldnae have seen me for dust," said Lamby. "Ma arse would've been a blur on the horizon."

"The worst was tae come." McAlpine knew he had most of his audience captivated as he took another drink in order to steady his nerves. "I managed tae get tae the wall an' that was where I found Alec. He was shakin' like a leaf havin' realised that although we'd managed tae get in tae the graveyard, there didnae appear tae be any way oot."

"Ye mean ye were trapped?" asked Marjorie.

McAlpine nodded. "That we were. Trapped; stuck in there wi' that monster that had just eaten, well I presume eaten, the two Tucker boys. I'll confess I was fair shittin' maself, more so when, through the smoke, I saw that thing comin' towards us. I'm no' kiddin' ye, it was like a demon from Hell, an' that's no exaggeration."

"*Demon from Hell?* Bah! From yer description it just sounds like a perv in a black coat just back from the dentist," added Hannah, unable, despite his earlier warning, to contain his sarcasm.

McAlpine rose from his seat, fists clenched. "Are ye sayin' I'm a liar? Ye bastard, that ye are! I'll take ye ootside an give ye a good seein' tae, so I will!"

"Steady on, the pair o' ye!" said Shug. He pointed a finger at Hannah. "That's yer last warnin', Tam. Any more—"

"Ach, bugger it! I didnae come in here the night tae listen tae this shite, free drinks or not." Disgruntled, Hannah got to his feet, drained his glass, got his coat and stomped angrily out of the pub, slamming the door behind him.

"Now that that arsehole's gone, I want tae know what happened next," said Dixon.

"There was nothin' for it but tae split up. I ran one way an' Alec went the other. I guess I was the lucky one that day, for the thing, an' the more I think aboot it, the more I'm inclined tae believe it *was* a vampire, went after Alec. I reached a side gate an' found maself in Caledonia Street. It was there that I bumped intae ma cousin, Burnie. After tellin' him what had happened we ran home but as there was naeb'dy in, we went tae the school an' told the heidmaster. O' course, he didnae believe any o' it, but the weans…well."

* * * *

"Christ…the things ye find yerself daein' these days," muttered Lamby. Drinking from a can of *Tennent's*, he walked alongside McAlpine at the head of the small group as they made their way through the thickening fog and drizzle towards the Southern Necropolis.

McAlpine threw his cigarette to the ground and nodded his agreement. Only ten minutes ago he had been drinking in the relative comfort of *Dirty Betty's* and now here he was, leading Lamby, Reed, Dixon and 'One-Armed Bob' down the rat-infested streets.

When the Cambridge professor had suggested paying a nocturnal visit to the graveyard at the centre of their conversation his idea had initially been vociferously declined; that was until the man's wallet had come out. He had offered anyone who would accompany him to the place a crisp twenty-pound note as well as a four-can carry-out or a bottle of their choice—only Marjorie and Shug had declined his proposal.

McAlpine glanced over his shoulder, noticing that Reed and the other two were out of earshot. "It wouldnae have been so bad if he'd decided tae visit it in the mornin'. All this crap aboot wantin' tae experience the feel o' the place doesnae sit well wi' me."

"Same here," Lamby agreed. "Still, all we have tae dae is show him the cemetery, wait ten minutes or so an' then clear off. It's easy enough money."

"We could always just mug him." McAlpine grinned. "Beat him up. Grab his wallet an' tie him tae a lamppost."

Lamby laughed then took another drink from his can.

"Ye're goin' the wrong way!" Dixon called out. "It's quicker goin' doon this snicket."

McAlpine and Lamby headed back. Re-joining the main group, they all set off down the narrow pathway which wended through a new social housing development. In daylight, the area was relatively safe but when the sun went down it became rife with denizens for whom antisocial behaviour was a way of life. Old sofas, a couple of battered cars, overflowing wheelie bins, buckled shopping trolleys, torn plastic bags and all manner of domestic rubbish formed a large midden in a central square.

The shadowy gloom seemed to compress around them.

"Once we get across the main road we'll be at the gatehouse," said Dixon.

Reaching into a jacket pocket, McAlpine took out a small battery-operated torch and switched it on. Now that they were nearing the entrance to the Southern Necropolis, he began to feel uneasy. He felt his mind beginning to waver as a tiny shaking tremor in his legs set in. If only he could push away the idea that there was something in the dark; a half-seen thing lurking somewhere in the shadows around him, he would feel a little better. But try as he would, he could not exorcise the things on his mind; awful things that bunched the muscles of his stomach, tightening them into hard knots of fear, sending his heart racing in an uneven rhythm in his chest. He felt sick. With a mental effort, he pulled himself together, drew in a deep breath and plodded forward.

Swathes of fog dispersed on a gust of wind as, spectrally, the sandstone built gatehouse to the Southern Necropolis loomed before them.

"So, this is where it all happened." There was a measurement of awe in Reed's voice as he moved to the front of the group.

"Christ! Look at us!" said Lamby, addressing the others. "Five grown men stood oot here gettin' soaked when we should be inside gettin' pissed or watchin' the telly. If the polis saw us they'd wonder what the hell we were up tae."

"Grave robbin', probably," Dixon added.

"Or vampire huntin'," Lamby replied. "An' tae tell you the truth I'd be happier if I did have a cross an' some garlic."

"At least we've got the holy water." McAlpine delved into a coat pocket, took out his whisky bottle and unscrewed the lid. He took a swig, savouring the burn of the raw liquor as it went down his throat.

"Gentlemen, may we…?" Reed prompted, gesturing towards the gateway.

"Ho'd up a minute. I need a pish." Dixon unzipped and urinated against the arched entrance.

There was an eeriness here that made McAlpine's skin crawl. For fifty years he had purposefully avoided entering this place, the memories of what had occurred herein ensuring that he stayed well away. A sudden wave of horrible, grisly images, no doubt triggered by Reed's information that there had once been a leper colony nearby, assaulted his mind. Ghastly, cowled, maggot-infested, decaying figures; some shambling, some pushed along in carts—all leaking, dripping and limbless—seemed to crowd in. *Gory bells*—the phrase played darkly on his mind, instilling thoughts of beings reduced to gelatinous, raw, lumps of putrid flesh plodding in a line like doomed monks to the grim tolling of an ancient bell. He stumbled, managing to stop himself from a fall with an outstretched hand.

Unlike the Gorbals, which had seen a large amount of modernisation over the past five decades, the Southern Necropolis had witnessed little change. Over a quarter of a million had been buried herein, many of the dead having lived lives of utter poverty and famine and as the group passed amongst the rows of weathered headstones it was nigh on impossible not to feel something of their presence. It was like a deathly hush—a sensation of torment and anguish which cried out from beyond the grave. It was as though the suffering went on for those interred herein.

Hedge-bordered avenues led off in three directions: to the left, right, and straight ahead.

"This is a bad idea," said McAlpine. He turned to Reed. "Is that it? Have ye seen enough?"

"Where exactly did you see that fiend?" Reed answered.

McAlpine shone the torchlight down the right-hand path. "I think it was somewhere along there. But…maybe it'd be best if we—"

"Ach, come on, John," said Dixon. "At least take the man tae where ye saw this thing, after all there's nothin' tae be worried aboot. The worst that could happen would be for us tae bump intae a group o' druggies an' even if we did, I think there's enough o' us tae scare them away."

McAlpine knew better. After all, he had been here all those years ago. He had seen that thing emerge from the fog and snatch the two Tucker boys, neither of whom were ever seen again despite an intensive police search. In addition to which, something seriously disturbing had befallen Foster, aging him terribly and rendering him a mindless cretin.

"I too am beginnin' tae think we shouldnae have come here," said Lamby. "This place is givin' me the screamin' abdabs."

"Well, I suppose we've come this far." Muttering under his breath, reluctantly McAlpine led the group deeper into the fog-wreathed burial ground, passing the countless weathered headstones and the occasional ivy-festooned marble statue. He stopped abruptly, sensing that something other than themselves was moving around in the darkness. He thought he could hear a sound—one that built itself up from a low whimpering whisper to a dismal moan before fading away. Flashing the torch from side to side, he stared wide-eyed into the gloom. "Christ! What was that?"

"What is it, John?" Lamby asked nervously.

"Shhh!" McAlpine brought a finger to his lips, signalling the group to be silent. "Listen!" For several moments the quietude bore down on him like a lead weight; the utter stillness playing havoc with his senses, filling him with a fear that crept like ice through his veins. He felt a tight clenching around his chest and thought for a moment that he was going to have another heart attack.

Twenty seconds ticked past.

The pain in McAlpine's chest subsided. He walked on for fifty yards or so. It was because he *had* seen that thing in the flesh that he had not accompanied the juvenile monster hunters who had later stormed the graveyard, much like the vengeful peasants with their pitchforks and burning torches often depicted in the old black and white horror films. Still, he found himself imaging the scene with utmost clarity. Subsequent photographs and news articles had depicted the children scaling the outer walls and streaming through the main gate, leaving a trail of vandalism and destruction in their wake.

"So, this…'vampire' wi' the metal teeth. This is where ye saw it?" Dixon asked.

"Aye, it was aboot here." McAlpine shivered. "I think this is the very spot. Christ! It's weird bein' back here, it really is."

"Would you say you're experiencing anything unnatural?" Reed inquired.

"I might be. It's hard tae...*Holy Christ! What the hell's that?*" McAlpine yelled as, with an alarming suddenness, an ethereal child's chalk-white face emerged from a covered grave less than a foot away as though it had just emerged through a gap in a dark velvet curtain. A hand appeared and then the phantom was pulling itself free, dragging its way out of the ground.

Groaning, a second, slightly smaller child-wraith crawled from beneath the dank turf. A worm slithered from an empty eye socket.

"No! No!" McAlpine screamed, backing away. He threw his whisky bottle at the nearest spirit but it passed straight though its incorporeal form and smashed off a headstone.

Reed, Dixon and Lamby stood confused, unable to see or hear the spectres.

"Killed us! Murdered us!" the ghosts of Ralphie and Pat Tucker wailed. Arms outstretched, the two apparitions glided forward, dressed in their ragged school uniforms of fifty years ago.

"I didnae dae it! I may've ran but I didnae kill ye! It was Alec who..." Paralysed with terror, McAlpine felt his throat seize up. Unable to breathe, he staggered, then fell to his knees, the torch falling from his shaking hand. There then followed a deathly, freezing sensation as the ghost of the younger boy passed through him. And in that moment, he knew that it was because he himself had 'died' twice on the operating table that he was able to see them—his own, admittedly brief, experience with the afterlife linking him to these two doomed unfortunates.

Someone else in the group could see them—'One-Armed Bob'; not because he had ever crossed over to the other side, but because it was *he* who had murdered the two young boys and then buried them nearby. It had been *he* who had dressed up as the notorious iron-toothed vampire that September day back in 1954, his years since spent as a drifter, a paedophile and a fruit machine-obsessed semi-alcoholic. In his younger days, his evil, sadistic and depraved behaviour had even brushed off on one of his more notorious neighbours and alleged devotees—Ian Brady.

Lamby and Dixon went to help McAlpine whilst Reed picked up the torch.

'One-Armed Bob' stumbled back, futilely waving his arms to stave off the ghastly revenants. He turned to run, but his tired and aged legs only carried him a few yards before he fell face first onto the path.

"Can ye no' see them; the ghosts?" McAlpine cried out loudly.

"What're ye on aboot?" Dixon answered.

"Jesus Christ!" shouted Lamby. "What's up wi' 'Bob'?"

In the torchlight, McAlpine could see that the two vengeful entities were punching, kicking and stomping on the old man, causing him to writhe and cry out in pain.

"Is he having a fit?" Reed asked.

Lamby moved to help 'One-Armed Bob' and then drew back suddenly upon seeing the obscene patches of greenish-white slime that now covered parts of him. "What the…?"

"Good God! I think that's…ectoplasm!" Reed directed the torch on the squirming victim.

McAlpine wanted to avert his eyes but stronger was the morbid fascination which compelled him to watch the unearthly assault.

Had these attacks been purely physical then, even given the size and strength of the assailants, the old man would either be dead or at the least grievously injured. His false teeth fell out—proper dentures this time, not the gimmicky, grey-painted plastic fangs he had bought long ago from a joke shop. His remaining hair fell out and the skin on his face tightened, becoming cadaverous. Knobbly hands became almost skeletal and his whole frame began to cave-in; his once fine-fitting jacket and trousers now over-baggy and slime-spattered.

Lamby threw up.

Dixon ran screaming into the darkness.

"We should get an ambulance!" Reed said.

"I think it's too late for that." McAlpine wanted to flee—to get as far from this cursed place as he possibly could but a strange desire to see this unearthly act of retribution through to its conclusion held him in place. This was justice—Gorbals' style—harsh, brutal and unforgiving.

The attack on 'One-Armed Bob' lasted little more than ninety seconds. That he was still alive bordered on the miraculous, although, given the condition he was left in, it would have been far better for him if he had died. Practically excarnated, he had been reduced to little more than a living skeleton, much of the flesh from his bones having been psychically skinned. His eyes resembled egg whites; vacuous—as though he had been stripped of his soul. The years he had stolen from the two young boys were transferred to him, aging him horribly. Gibbering insanely, drool leaking from his almost non-existent lips, the bare husk of a man began crawling, arthritically, on all fours.

With a mournful cry, their vengeance complete, the phantom Tucker boys vanished.

Three

From the Darkside of the Dreamtime

It was a late summer afternoon and the Western Australian road—more track than actual roadway—was surrounded on all sides by a vastness of rocky desert, which stretched and shimmered like a mirage for as far as the eye could see. Apart from the muted rumble of thunder on the southern horizon, there was an absolute quietness that, like the stifling heat, seemed to wrap itself around the battered, green van.

"I don't know about you, but I can't help but think something terrible happened back there." Forty-one-year-old anthropologist, John Booth, grasped the steering wheel tightly and looked into his rearview mirror. Through the cloud of dust kicked up by the vehicle's tyres, he watched as the overturned car faded into the distance. The fact that no passengers had been found and yet it was abundantly clear that a violent struggle had taken place was deeply unsettling. There had been numerous splashes of blood. From the personal effects found scattered throughout, it appeared that the car belonged to a Perth-based art collector called Dwight Turner. A photograph showed a bespectacled, fairly non-descript man stood alongside a rather plump woman, presumably his wife, and two teenage kids: a fair-haired girl and a dark-haired boy.

Brian Murdoch, the man in the passenger seat, cracked open a can of lager and took a hearty swallow.

"What do you reckon? You think those folks might've been attacked by a pack of dingoes?" Booth asked.

"No way. I've never known of dingoes to cause that kind of carnage. Besides, it would've taken something mighty big to turn that car over. And those tracks...they were like nothing I've ever seen before. Just doesn't make sense."

"What're you thinking then?"

"I don't know."

Booth concentrated on driving, an intentness to his eyes as he scanned the great expanse of arid wilderness. He lived and lectured in Perth, working in a museum where his main focus of study was aboriginal rock art. Having heard rumours of the discovery of strange, hitherto unidentified, petroglyphs, he had been assigned to venture out here in order to locate and record them. He knew that this was a harsh and unforgiving land, criss-crossed by hundreds of barely navigable trails that led to places no one sane would care to go. "We have to inform the authorities. But first we have to reach somewhere. I'm worried that we haven't seen any signposts for some time. Where's the closest town?"

"*Town?* You're having a laugh, aren't you? There are no towns round here. Nearest settlement would be Warburton and that's back along the Gunbarrel Highway. Two hundred kilometres or more. We might as well be on the Moon." Murdoch finished his drink, crushed his can and nonchalantly tossed it over his right shoulder onto the back seat. He rummaged around for the map and opened it up. After a moment's consultation, he looked up. "You know, I hate to say this but I'm beginning to think we might've taken the wrong turning."

"*What!?* You're supposed to be the guide. I thought you knew where we were going!"

"I did. Until we reached that junction and I asked that one-eyed abo for directions. Guess the old bastard thought he'd have some fun and send us the wrong way. I had a bad feeling about him from the moment I clapped eyes on him."

Booth had an uneasy feeling that his companion was right. "Surely we can't go on and on without coming to somewhere?"

"Well, like I said, don't be expecting to find anywhere soon. Hell, the driveways of some of the ranchers I know who've got property out this way are over fifty kilometres long. You young city-folk have no real concept of distance. Providing you had the fuel, you could drive non-stop for a day and a half out here and not see another living soul or anything remotely approaching civilisation."

"So do we—?" Booth stamped down heavily on the brakes, bringing the van to a stop so sudden that it stalled as a large, scrawny creature, its fur mangy and covered in unsightly, maggot-infested sores, sprang into the path of the van. It looked up, its eyes blood-filled and bulging from their sockets, before springing into the brush on the opposite side of the road.

"Bloody kangaroo. Looked all skin and bones. Diseased, maybe?" voiced Murdoch.

Nerves afire, Booth watched as the terribly gaunt marsupial painfully bounded away. His eyes widened as three more emaciated, ghastly-looking kangaroos leapt past, almost as though they were fleeing something. He turned the ignition key. The overheated engine stuttered, stirred to life and then cut out. He tried again, applying greater pressure on the accelerator. A series of bone-jarring rattles shook the van as it lurched forward a few metres and then stopped. Dead. He turned to his companion. "How good a mechanic are you?"

"Bloody useless, I'm afraid."

Repeatedly, Booth tried to get the van working. "Come on you bastard!" He was getting angry. He gave the key a fierce twist and it snapped in two. "Christ! That's bloody great that is!" Throwing open the door, he got out and slammed a fist onto the steaming bonnet. Swearing loudly, he began kicking the nearest tyre.

"I'd stop doing that if I were you," advised Murdoch. He had his hat on and stood nearby.

"Okay." Breathing heavily, Booth stepped back from the van. "So now what are we going to do?" Despite the fact that he was trying to remain calm, there was desperation, bordering on panic in his words.

"Assuming we can't get the van going we've got two options." Murdoch counted them on a thumb and forefinger. "One—we stay here until someone comes along although God knows how long a wait that might be, or two—we go walkabout."

Squinting his eyes against the glare, Booth scanned the horizon for anything hospitable looking. There was nothing but death out there, of that he was certain. Hot, burning, agonising death—whether due to dehydration, starvation, sunstroke or a multitude of venomous insects, arachnids and reptiles, in addition to whatever had wrought such terrible violence against the unfortunates they had passed earlier.

"No doubt you're thinking it'd be better to stay with the van," said Murdoch, correctly reading the anthropologist's thoughts. "Normally I'd agree with you but seeing as *something* happened to those poor buggers in the car, I think it's be better if we got moving. There's something just not right about this place that's beginning to gnaw at my nerves."

Booth frowned. "What do you mean?"

"To be honest, I'm not sure." There was a strange expression on Murdoch's heavily tanned, rugged features that made him look a lot older than his sixty-three years.

"If you've got something on your mind, I want to hear it."

"There are lots of legends about these places that I guess don't reach the big cities. Why, I reckon even a man of learning such as yourself, someone whose got an interest in such things, has heard only a fraction of the old stories. There are some places out here that even the abos avoid. And with bloody good reason."

The sensation of restless apprehension that had been growing in Booth's mind all day, and more so since discovering the wrecked car, was now solidifying into something more definite, more imminent. It was as though the utter stillness and desertion around him was peopled with soundless, half-noticed things that flitted on the edge of his vision, moving swiftly and soundlessly in the silence. A sick sensation of impending disaster began to take hold of him, stirring in the far depths of his mind.

"There's something wrong about this trail," said Murdoch. Crouching down, he scooped up a handful of sand and grit and sifted it through his clenched fist. "I thought at first it was just my overwrought imagination, but now I'm not so sure. I've a feeling of something…something evil."

"*Evil?* What do you mean?"

Murdoch swatted at a fly on the nape of his neck. "I've spent most of my life in the outback, Mr Booth. I know all the wildlife and more importantly how to survive out here but there's a bad feel to this place." He sniffed the air. "There's a foul smell in the air. Something rotten."

Booth could smell nothing untoward. He opened his mouth to speak when his eye caught a glimpse of something far ahead, further along the trail. "What that?" he asked, pointing.

Murdoch got to his feet and walked forward a few paces.

"Can you make it out?"

Murdoch grinned cheerily. He paced over and gave his companion a friendly smack on the shoulder. "Could be we're in luck. Come on, let's pack what water there is and see what's what. Think I'll also bring 'Barry' along just for a bit of protection. Might need him if we have to do a bit of hunting. Besides, you never know when snakes… specially those of the two-legged variety, might pop up." He went to the back of the van, opened the door and drew out several canteens of water and a *Savage Model 110* repeating bolt-action rifle which, along with a bandolier of cartridges, he slung over a shoulder.

"So what is it?" Booth shielded his eyes and peered. From this distance, it looked like an irregular heap of piled rocks—a small cairn.

"It's a route marker. The abos use them. Should tell us where we are." Straightening his hat, Murdoch strode off.

Booth was finding it hard to match the man who now marched off purposefully before him, his chiselled features burnt a leathery teak by years spent in this unforgiving wilderness, with the smartly dressed man he had first met a week ago in the museum back in Perth. He himself was a city-dweller and he was only too well aware that, without transportation or the ability to get in touch with the outside world, he was completely at the other's mercy. "Hold up!" he cried as he jogged off in pursuit.

Five minutes later they reached the heap of rocks, atop which perched a sun-bleached skull.

"That's human, isn't it? What does that mean?" asked Booth.

"It's not good, I'm afraid." Murdoch crouched down. He picked up the skull, removed the uppermost stone, examined it briefly, then placed it back atop the pile. "This ain't no route marker. It's a warning sign." Almost reverently, he replaced the skull.

"A warning sign?"

"Yeah, a warning sign." Murdoch stood up and looked around him as though half-expecting some imminent threat.

"I'm confused."

"You must've seen some of those old war movies with the 'Danger! Minefield!' signs. Well, this is something similar. Except, obviously there's no mines out here." Murdoch unslung his rifle. "Rather, it's something else."

A sudden fear struck at Booth with a savage, almost physical violence, knifing into his throat, constricting the muscles of his chest, forcing his heart into an uncertain, uneasy rhythm. He stared out through slitted eyes across the rugged wastes. Everywhere, it was the same. It made no difference in which direction he turned his head.

It was a scorching, mind-shrivelling hell.

"Seeing as the van's not going anywhere, why don't we head back to the car?" Booth suggested. "I noticed that the keys were still in the ignition. Providing there's no real damage, if we can flip it over, we might be able to get it started. It's not like we're stealing it. After all, I can't see the owners coming back any time soon, can you? If questioned, we'll just tell the truth and say that—"

"Christ! Look at that!" Murdoch interrupted. His eyes were fixed on a point five hundred metres or so distant. "It looks like a mini cyclone…heading right for us. It's moving fast! Come on, let's get back to the van." He turned, his fast walk quickly becoming a full-out sprint.

Booth ran after the guide. Within seconds, he could hear the savage howling of the approaching tornado. To him, it seemed as though the sky had changed colour. No longer was it a brilliant blue-white. Instead, it was a dark, ominous hue; shadowy and filled with twisting, boiling shapes—a whirling cloud that moved rapidly towards them, scudding over the very tops of the rocky crags and the up-thrusting dunes, filled with whirlwinds of airborne grit and stinging sand. Throwing the van door open, he scrambled inside, slamming it shut behind him. He thought he could hear something snarling.

"What the hell is that?" Murdoch stared out of the passenger window, his eyes fixed on the rapidly advancing black vortex.

Booth was about to respond when a dense mass of whipped-up sand and grit fell on the windscreen, soon obscuring all view and plunging them into darkness. Panic threatened to take hold and several seconds passed before he realised that he was holding his breath as though subconsciously fearful that whatever had caused this strange phenomenon was toxic in origin—like the sulphurous gases and volcanic tephra which had spewed from Vesuvius, poisoning and burying thousands in ancient Pompeii. He gulped nervously, only vaguely aware that his companion was fumbling with a box of matches.

Light from the small flickering flame cast Murdoch's normally healthy-looking face into a ghastly pallor. Wide-eyed, he peered around him in the shadowy darkness. "This ain't no normal—" He stopped abruptly at the sound of a heavy thump on the van's roof.

Booth's heart lurched.

Murdoch's match burnt out. Hastily, he struck another. No sooner had he done so when there came what sounded like the bare-footed patter of feet on the metal surface mere inches above his head. This was followed by a scrabbling commotion from his side of the van as though a pack of rats was trying to get in, prompting him to shrink back in his seat.

The snuffling, scratching noise got louder.

The light from the match looked feeble in Murdoch's trembling fingers.

Suddenly, the unnerving sound ceased. Everything was quiet. Silence seemed to press itself down tightly against them.

For a terrible moment, Booth felt unable to breathe. It was as though he was suffocating from the fear. A numbing terror crept through his body, clutching at his heart. It was how he imagined being buried alive would feel. And those weird sounds. What had caused them? At any moment, he dreaded to see something pale and grotesque press itself up against the windscreen. He took several deep breaths, aware that he was allowing his imagination to run riot. Mentally, he tried to put things into some kind of perspective; to restore reason and sanity. It was just a sandstorm, nothing more. The sounds had quite feasibly been caused by a kangaroo scrambling over the van.

There was a sudden, violent judder. It was followed seconds later by a dreadful growling sound.

Both men yelled as the van rocked to one side. The side Murdoch was on was raised higher. It then thumped back on to its tyres.

There then came a resounding bang on the roof and the whole vehicle began to shake from side to side.

"It's a bloody earthquake!" Murdoch shouted.

In his mind, Booth could picture the van teetering on the edge of a freshly opened fissure, the ground crumbling away as the earth threatened to swallow them down into its depths. He felt sick and to his alarm realised that he was shivering uncontrollably. He wanted to get out yet at the same time was filled with horror at the thought of what could be out there.

Murdoch was reaching for the door handle when something cracked against the windscreen causing it to splinter. A ferocious blast struck the van with enough force to pitch it over to one side.

Booth screamed.

And then the vehicle was turning again. It canted dangerously, then thumped back down.

Blood trickled from a shallow cut on Booth's forehead where he had hit the window, and he was in pain from having been crushed by his companion. He now lay sprawled, uncomfortably pinioned against the steering wheel and the windscreen. His mind was screaming at him to get out, to escape from this madness. Futilely, he pushed at the door, but it would not budge.

Groaning, Murdoch managed to extricate his left foot which had become trapped under his seat. Cursing volubly, he shifted his position and kicked out at the windscreen. Savagely, he booted it again and again.

Booth could smell gasoline. He began to panic. Fear leant him strength and he too began to hammer at the glass believing that the vehicle was liable to explode at any moment. In the darkness, he felt around for anything of use, his fingers clenching around the firm handle of a heavy wrench. He was just about to crack it against the glass, when he noticed that not only was everything now still and quiet, but that the darkness seemed to be receding, evaporating almost. Splotches of sunlight began to form before his eyes.

Murdoch noticed it too.

Shafts of searing hot, welcome sunlight speared into the interior. Soon the black cloud and the nightmare it had brought in its wake had vanished completely.

Dashing the wrench against the windscreen, Booth shattered the glass. Knocking aside the remaining shards, he crawled out, Murdoch, gripping his rifle, right behind him.

On bleeding hands and grazed knees, the two men dragged themselves further, before clambering to their feet and moving well clear of the over-turned van.

"What the hell was that?" said Booth, rubbing his right shoulder. "And where'd it go?"

"I don't know, but come have a look at this." Murdoch strode over to where several grisly, unidentifiable pieces of bloody meat and bones lay. It looked like roadkill.

"What the hell's that?"

Murdoch crouched down in order to examine the gore. "Looks like bits of kangaroo. It's hard to tell but there appears to be claw-marks."

"Claw-marks?" Booth did not like the sound of that. His uneasiness increased. He turned his sight to their surroundings, hoping against hope that whatever had recently attacked the van had now gone for good. All was still, unnaturally so and he was just about to suggest to Murdoch that they get moving when, suddenly, a small, fair-haired head popped up from behind a large rock some fifty metres away.

It was a teenage girl.

"That's the young Sheila in the photograph. We've got to help her." Booth made his way across the stretch of desert. Scrambling over the broken ground and getting scratched from the wiry bushes, he edged into the narrow crevice between two boulders in which the young girl had been hiding.

Her denim shorts and white T-shirt with a faded *Coca-Cola* design on it were scuffed and torn but she herself appeared uninjured—physically at least. However, her trembling and the haunted, tearful look in her pale blue eyes conveyed a different story regarding the mental ordeals she had endured.

"There's no need to worry." Booth gripped her gently but firmly by her thin shoulders, aware that she was in shock. "Everything's going to be all right. I promise."

Murdoch scrambled over. "She's scared half to death."

"My mum and...dad...are gone. My brother..." the girl mumbled, her eyes vacant. She began to sway on her feet.

"Shhh...you're okay now," said Murdoch.

"What are we going to do?" Booth asked. Gently, he cradled the girl, lowering her to the ground, aware that she was on the verge of passing out.

"I'll think of something." Murdoch ran an expert eye over his rifle, checking to make sure it had not been damaged. He then handed it to the anthropologist. "You take this."

Booth looked confused.

"We can't stay here so I'm going to have at little look about; see if there's anything that we can use to our advantage. While I'm gone, stay out of the sun for you could fry an egg on these rocks and try not to make any noise."

"Splitting up? Is that a good idea?"

"I'm not going to be gone long. Thirty minutes or so. I'm just going to scout around. I'll also get water and supplies from the van. If I get the chance, I'll make it to the car; see if there's any way of using it to get out of here."

"And what if that thing comes back?"

"Then I guess we're buggered." With no further words, Murdoch grinned, straightened his hat and determinedly strode off.

* * * *

Even though Booth was sat in the shadow of a large rock, he found the heat unbearable. His skin was beginning to prickle, and it felt as though his brain was cooking. His throat was parched, and breathing was becoming harsh and painful as though with each shallow inhalation he was taking in a lungful of hot dust. Matters were made worse by the knowledge that, not far away, in the van, were several canteens of water. Yet he lacked the courage to venture from this relatively safe place of concealment in order to get them and satiate his thirst.

Moaning occasionally, the girl shifted in her sleep.

Booth looked again at his watch. It was now ten past six. Murdoch had been gone for fifty-five minutes and with each minute that ticked by he could not help but feel that, despite his wilderness survival skills, something terrible had befallen the outdoorsman. There was something unnatural out there, of that he had little doubt. He found himself wondering just what he would do if it were to suddenly appear. He was a reasonable shot with a rifle but just how effective would that be against something which appeared to lack a physical form? His mind drifted to the girl, wondering what her story was— wondering if, once she awoke, she would be able to provide any useful information. Where were her other family members? Were they alive? How had she managed to escape?

Eyes shut, the girl began mumbling incoherently.

Booth wished there was something he could do, but aside from waking her there was little to ease her suffering. He felt utterly helpless and just sitting here, waiting for Murdoch to return, was playing havoc with his mind. He knew that if some calamity had befallen his companion, then the chances of either him or the girl getting out of this alive were greatly reduced, for he had no expertise in surviving in these conditions.

"I'm back."

With a start, Booth turned, relieved to see Murdoch standing above on the rock. "Christ. Took your time, didn't you?"

Ignoring the question, Murdoch stepped away, disappearing briefly, before reappearing from the side of the rock. He carried a rucksack in one hand and had another on his back. "Well, do you want the good news or the bad news?"

Booth tutted. "What's the good news?"

The two rucksacks were now on the ground and Murdoch was rummaging through one of them. Removing a can of lager, he cracked it open, took a drink and then, tiredly, sat down. "There's food and water here to last us a couple of days, more if we ration it. Also, there's an old mine just beyond that ridge to the north; ten-minute walk from here. Looks a good place to hide and rest up."

"The bad news?"

Murdoch gave a heavy sigh, his face grim. "I…I think I found what's left of the girl's family." He raised the can to his lips once more then took off his hat and rolled the relatively cool metal on his forehead.

Booth sat up.

"About fifty metres from the car, which I don't think there's a cat in hell's chance of getting started, there's…" Murdoch winced. "Suffice to say, it would appear that the poor bastards have been partially eaten. What confuses me, however, is the tracks. What starts out as an obvious and easy to follow trail of disturbed ground, like that caused by a small twister, abruptly changes."

"Changes? Into what?"

Murdoch finished his drink, crushed the can and put it to one side. "Bare, human footprints."

* * * *

Booth sat just inside the entrance to the mine, watching as the sun sank beyond the western ridge, the lengthening shadows seeming to flow across the rugged landscape like a dark menace. There had been no more sightings of that unexplainable whirlwind, although he knew it would be foolish to assume that it had gone for good. "It's so quiet," he muttered.

"Too quiet." Rifle in hand, Murdoch gazed skyward.

"Still, it should enable her to get some sleep. Hopefully when she wakes, she'll be less traumatised and she'll able to tell us a bit more about what happened. Poor girl's hardly said a word since we found her."

Murdoch nodded and turned to look where the girl lay, gently snoring.

"Who do you reckon built this mine?"

"Not the abos, that's for sure." Murdoch appraised the timber tunnel supports, none of which looked particularly safe. "Given the pretty basic level of workmanship, I'd guess it was a team of early, maybe Victorian, prospectors. Used to get groups of them out here, scouring the creeks and sinking shafts wherever they thought they could extract some gold. Made some rich. Made many more poor. A hard, challenging life, no doubt about that. Strange that there doesn't appear to be any outer buildings, not even the remains of any."

"You think this was a gold mine?"

"Definitely."

"How far back do you think it goes?" Booth stared into the tunnel; the uneven floor with its length of rail, the wooden joists and the hewn walls visible for thirty feet or so before disappearing into an unwelcoming darkness. At the fringe of the shadowy gloom, he could just about discern an overturned mine car.

"A hundred feet, maybe more. There could be many adjoining tunnels as well."

Booth checked his watch. "Nearly nine. We've been here for over two hours and no sign of that thing."

"That doesn't mean it's not out there. It could be waiting, watching."

"You realising you're assigning a level of intelligence to something which, at the end of the day, may be nothing more than...I don't know, a swarm of locusts."

"Do you think it was a swarm of locusts that carried off and devoured the Turners? And what about the footprints?"

"So, what do we do? We can't stay here for ever. We can't even see the road from here to flag down anyone."

"Not good, is it?"

"Is that all you can say?" There was anger in Booth's voice.

"What do you want me to say?"

"I don't know. You're the expert...the outdoorsman." Booth exhaled deeply. This was becoming nightmarish. Shaking his head, he found himself accepting the realisation that it could be that this was a situation he may not survive. Wild animals he could deal with—for they could be shot and killed. Likewise lawless people. But this... just what in God's name was it?

Murdoch took a cigar from a shirt pocket and bit off the end. "I've been wracking my brain to try and think as to just what this thing is and the only thing, I keep coming up with is that it's, well... you're not going to like what I'm about to say." He struck a match and lit up.

"I'm listening."

"I know you're a man of learning, Mr Booth, and that you know quite a bit about the old abo legends but it's one thing reading about them in books and quite something else to hear them spoken. Words and stories take on a whole new meaning when you're out here, far from the libraries in the big cities. They become real. And...whilst some of the stories, in fact most of them, are pleasant to hear...there are others. Ones which, well, let's just say, aren't so nice. If you were to delve deep into the mysticism of the Dreamtime, you'd find lots of cases of monsters and demons; baby-eating giants, shapeshifters, vampires, snake-people and Christ knows what else."

"I'm aware of that, but it's just myth. They're creation stories handed down through the generations; told by the tribal elders to—"

"And that thing out there? That thing that threw the van around like a rag doll and slaughtered those folk? Is that just a myth?"

"So, what are you saying?" Booth crossed his arms. "You think that it's some kind of aborigine devil?"

Murdoch shrugged his shoulders. "You probably don't know, and now's probably not the best time to tell you, but it's rumoured that, hundreds, if not thousands, of years ago, this area used to be settled by the *Walamaga People*—a nasty bunch of bastards that practiced cannibalism, human sacrifice and devil-worship. Legend has it that places like this are known to retain a deep, dark, ancestral force—a thing best buried and forgotten. However, it can sometimes make its way to the surface."

"This is crazy. Horror film stuff. But let's assume for a moment you're right and that some ancient evil has been awoken. How do we fight it?"

"Fire might work."

"Yeah, might work. Might be of no bloody good either, except for drawing its attention. And there's no way—"

"I'd stay still, if I were you."

"Why?" Following the direction of Murdoch's pointing finger, Booth slowly tilted his head. Eyes widening with fear, lips trembling, he found himself almost face to face with a large black spider which had crawled from a crevice in the mine wall and was currently on his left shoulder, less than a finger's length from his bare neck. Sweat instantly broke out on his brow upon seeing the scarlet streak down its bulbous, glossy black abdomen. He had the horrible impression that it was looking straight at him.

"It's a female redback. Biggest bastard I've ever seen."

Booth went rigid, paralysed with terror. Redbacks were as nasty as funnelwebs and with no anti-venom on hand a bite could prove fatal.

"Okay, just stay calm." Murdoch reached into a jacket pocket for his leather gloves. Putting one on his right hand, he edged forward, positioned himself, then, with the speed of a striking cobra, he reached out and grabbed the highly venomous arachnid. In another sudden move, he dashed it to the ground.

Booth breathed a sigh of relief as he watched the eight-legged creature skitter under a rock. He rose to his feet, well aware that where there was one there was likely to be others but fortunately for him there were none to be seen.

"Better just check there aren't any crawling on the young woman over there," said Murdoch. He went over to where she lay.

"We can't stay here."

"I know." Having ensured there were no spiders on the girl, Murdoch went to the mine entrance and peered out into the darkening daylight.

The sky was a vivid indigo-blue with patches of black clouds which blotted out many of the brilliant stars.

"Do you think we should risk trying to get to the road?" Booth asked.

Murdoch scratched at the rough stubble on his chin. Inwardly, he was weighing things up; bringing his years of experience in this harsh land to the fore. He knew how to avoid and deal with the numerous nasty critters that made this place their home; knew how to get water from mallee eucalyptus roots, sub-strata creeks and solar stills; knew how to forage for bush tucker—how to skin, prepare and cook desert game. Contrary to the answer he had previously given to Booth, providing that dark mass did not attack them, they could remain holed up here for a long time. However, it would be far from pleasant.

"Look. If we're going to make a go for the road, we're going to have to do it now."

"I don't think that's a good idea. No doubt you think otherwise, but I reckon it's best if we rest up here for the night. For the time being, we're safe. I'll get a fire going and then I think we should venture a little deeper into the mine; get away from the entrance so as not to be seen. Who knows, if we're lucky, we might find something of use back there."

"Like what?"

"Don't know till you look. Dynamite, maybe?"

"If there's any dynamite down there, you'd be best not to go near it. Old dynamite leaches nitro glycerine and is incredibly unstable."

"We can't sit here any longer. We'd better go further back."

Booth was unconvinced. "Christ. This is going from bad to worse. There could be anything down there."

"I think it's a risk we're going to have to take." From a sheath at his belt, Murdoch took his large, serrated, huntsman's knife and proceed to trim long splinters from the nearest wooden prop. Gathering them up, he tied them into a bundle with a piece of cotton cut from his shirt. He went to the periphery of the shadowy interior and, using his matches, soon had a small fire going.

In the welcome glow, Booth could see that the mine extended another ten metres or so before fading into deep darkness once more. The overturned mine car he had seen earlier lay rusty and empty.

Cautiously, Murdoch made his way deeper into the mine, his boots crunching on the loose rocks. There were many webs, some teeming with spiderlings but most were high up, spanning the corners where the roof supports reached the ceiling. On the ground, amidst the rubble and bits of junk, he saw some items which could prove of use: a shovel, a coil of rope, an old frying pan, and a pickaxe handle. Hanging from a hook was an old miner's lamp.

Booth came forward. "Anything?"

"Not really." Having discovered that there was no oil in the lamp, Murdoch picked up the old frying pan. "You on for seeing what's further back?"

Reluctantly, Booth nodded. "Suppose so."

"Good." Placing some of the burning splinters into the pan, Murdoch fashioned a crude, portable light source. Holding it out before him, he advanced, the makeshift torch doing something to illuminate his surroundings.

The tunnel walls narrowed.

"We shouldn't go too far," said Booth. "I don't think it's right that we leave the girl alone."

"Let's just see where it goes." Murdoch took a dozen steps and then stopped.

The way ahead was blocked by a huge pile of rubble; a cave-in which filled the entire tunnel. It looked totally impassable.

Examining the obstruction, Booth noticed a skeletal hand protruding from under a rock at the base of the collapsed tunnel. He crouched down in order to examine it, half-expecting to see it grasping an old scroll—a treasure map. Such a fanciful idea was torn instantly from his mind by the terrible, high-pitched scream which echoed down the tunnel.

"*Christ!*" Murdoch spun round. "What the hell was that?"

Booth gulped nervously. Whether due to the strange subterranean acoustics or the dreadfully confined space of the tunnel the wail had sounded unearthly; ghastly.

The scream came again; a desperate, tortured cry.

Booth was no hero. Although he knew the right thing to do was to retrace their steps and see what was happening, he could not get a particularly nasty image out of his head—that of the girl having transformed into some sort of hideous witch; her face grisly and cadaverous, her eyes blood-red, her hands clawed. And now she barred the exit. There was no way out. That was the overwhelming horror and the wild terror of it all. A madness tore at his brain, making it impossible to think properly. He began to tremble.

"*Mum!*" The screech was ear-splitting. "*Dad!*" From out of the darkness, the girl, her eyes filled with horror, ran towards them.

* * * *

The three of them sat huddled around the small fire twenty or so metres into the mine. Outside it was dark and the temperature had dropped sharply. Occasionally there came the mournful, pained howl of some lone creature but otherwise all was still and quiet.

Booth shook his head, his mind in turmoil, rebelling against what the girl, whose name it transpired was Angie, had told them. Vacantly, he watched the dancing flames, his mundane concepts of normality and reality having been stretched to the limit. It was insane, utter screaming madness! And yet, he saw nothing but sincerity in her eyes; no hint that any of this was fabrication. There was no doubt she was still distressed but she was no longer in a state of shock and her talking and actions had been far more rational than he would have expected, given the circumstances and having been told that her parents were dead.

Gently chewing his bottom lip, Murdoch too was lost in his own thoughts. He had said little and listened much, weighing things up. He had heard some mighty weird stories over the course of his life—tales that would instil fear into the hearts of all but the bravest—but this…

"It's true. You must believe me," Angie pleaded.

"It's bollocks. Nonsense. It has to be. I mean, how do you expect us to believe you? You're saying that…*thing*…out there is your *brother?*" The incredulity on Booth's face was blatant.

"Yes!" Angie answered. "Like I said, he was cursed as a baby."

"When your father accidently ran over and killed an old aborigine woman?" Booth said sceptically.

Angie nodded. "I know it sounds weird. It *is* weird. But we've lived with it for thirteen years. At first mum and dad didn't fully believe it either—didn't *want* to believe it. Then, as Mikey got older, they had to admit that there was something seriously wrong with him. I was seven, so Mikey would've been two, when he first changed. One minute he was playing with his toys on the floor, the next there came a loud cry and he'd turned into this wild creature; all fur and fangs. A small dark cloud formed around him. Next, he was violently spinning round, throwing chairs and things with the strength of a grown-up, tearing down the curtains. I remember dad rushing in and forcing Mikey back with a chair—like a lion-tamer at the circus. Somehow, he managed to pin him down, drag him to a cupboard and throw him inside. After ten minutes, Mikey began to cry and when my dad finally let him out he was normal. It was like nothing had happened. He changed once or twice during that year, then the transformations happened more often. There's no warning when it's going to happen, so it's not like…you know, werewolves and the full moon. Now that he's older, it's getting worse and it's lasting longer."

Disbelievingly, Booth shook his head and looked at Murdoch. "You don't buy this bullshit, do you?"

Murdoch shrugged his shoulders. "I don't know. It could be true… and it fits the evidence. Though I don't know how they could've kept it quiet."

"Mikey was kept away from other kids, and he never went to school. For most of his life, he was kept in a room my dad made in our basement. We…" Tears began to well up in Angie's eyes. "We live on a remote farm several kilometres outside Perth, and we hardly ever get visitors."

"Could you not go to the doctor? See a specialist?" Booth asked.

"My dad was certain they couldn't do anything for him. If anyone found out about him, he'd be killed, experimented on…or treated as a freak of nature. You've got to understand, when he's normal, he's kind, loving, highly-sensitive—as good a brother as any sister could hope to have. Both my parents loved him to bits."

And now, possibly because of him, they are in bits, Murdoch thought darkly.

"And this cure…?" Booth asked.

"It's the reason we came out here," Angie answered. "The hope that someone in the old woman's tribe will bring an end to the curse. After all, Mikey's innocent. He was just a baby at the time. If anyone was to blame it was my dad and now that…" She bowed her head in sorrow. Then, with a deep sigh, she looked up. "My dad made contact with one of the elders, a relative of the old woman and, as far as I know, an agreement was reached. It was a risk, bringing Mikey out in the car but there was nothing else for it. We hoped that just this once our luck would hold out. He was strapped in but that did nothing. I don't know how I managed to get away."

"Tell us again about the accident and the old aborigine woman," said Booth, fully aware his question sounded like the kind of probing inquiry the police used at interrogations to try and weed out lies and find inconsistencies.

Angie gave an exasperated sigh. "I was only five at the time, so I don't remember much about the actual accident, but I've been told what happened. My dad was driving me to school. Mikey was in the back, in his baby-seat. There was a rally or a protest of some sort being held by some aboriginal people at the City Hall and as a group of them were crossing the main road my dad, who had only recently passed his driving test, stepped on the accelerator instead of the brakes. At the last moment, he swerved, mounting the pavement. I remember a dreadful thud. Then screaming. For a time, everything went strange, like a dream—or a nightmare. Then the car door was opened, and I saw that old woman, covered in blood. She reached out, grabbed Mikey and gave this horrible, horrible cry. Although this was thirteen years ago, I can still see her face. Whenever I go to sleep, I see her. And I still see that bloody handprint she left on little Mikey's T-shirt—the one with *Taz*, the Tasmanian Devil, on it."

* * * *

Weird, brightly-coloured, psychedelic whorls, dots and kaleidoscopic patterns flashed intermittently and danced bizarrely; creating a mind-boggling phantasmagoria—one that, in his dream, Booth felt he could almost reach out and touch. Primordial motifs and symbols, some recognisable, but most defying any form of categorisation, swam briefly into view before vanishing completely. Pictures of strange, animal hybrids and stick men, the kind he had seen a hundred times depicted on ancient petroglyphs, weaved in and out of his troubled consciousness and somehow, he knew his mind was conjuring up his own awareness and mental concept of the Dreamtime.

Suddenly, almost as though triggered by that realisation, everything became grey and nebulous.

The surreal, illusory imagery assumed a more threatening aspect.

The world was now barren, bleak and monochrome—a wasteland; bled dry of life and colour.

In this nightmare place, Booth wandered—a lone, haggard figure, stumbling through a gaunt desolation. With each leaden step, his surroundings darkened. A dreadful, physical and mental exhaustion befell him; draining him, leaching him of what vitality he still possessed. Stubbornly, he walked on, drawn inexorably towards a low, rocky mound. On getting nearer, he saw that there were several small openings, around which lay piles of badly chewed bones.

From somewhere came the deep, disturbing, resonant drone of a didgeridoo.

To Booth's ears, it was an evil sound, one that instilled his dwindling sense of reality with grisly visions of monstrous, cannibalistic, half-human, half-beast abominations. From out of the burrows, dripped and poured rivulets of thick blood.

A tribal chant—ancient and wicked—rose from the very ground.

And then, from the openings, Booth saw them.

One, then two, then half a dozen. Black, scarred and scabbed whiskered snouts, matted with blood. The 'devils'—the world's largest carnivorous marsupials—scampered forth. Fang-filled mouths stretched wide to reveal ravenous, gaping maws. Snarling and emitting bloodcurdling screams, more and more now rushed from their warren. Most were entirely black, with a few having white streaks on their underbellies.

Booth froze. He stood, helplessly staring as the extremely aggressive creatures rushed towards him. And then they were upon him, teeth sinking deep into his calves, lacerating his trousers and shredding the meat from his legs. There was no pain, only the horrifying awareness that he was about to be eaten alive. He fell to the ground, whereupon the 'devils' swarmed over him, ferociously shaking him in their raptorial feeding frenzy. Teeth clamped around a wrist, sinking to the bone. His right hand was torn from his body and angrily squabbled over. Two of the beasts had gnawed into his stomach. Rear legs kicking and dislodging innards, they burrowed deeper. His face and one eye was ripped, grotesquely, from his skull.

* * * *

Shivering uncontrollably, Booth sprang awake, the horrors of the nightmare still vivid. Eyes staring, heart thumping, he sat up, temporarily disorientated, unaware as to where he was. "Jesus Christ!" He ran a hand over his brow, feeling the sheen of cold sweat.

From outside the mine, came the glow of daylight.

"So you be John Booth, eh?"

Booth turned on hearing his name spoken. By the light of the small fire, he saw a tall, lean figure.

"Good to see you've come through your first experience with *Jaku-Jimba*. Not all are so lucky."

"What?"

The stranger came forward.

Booth saw that the man was a thirty-something aborigine, clean-shaven and casually dressed in denim jeans and a T-shirt. There was a friendly sparkle in his deep brown eyes and his pearly smile. His skin was pure black.

"You can call me Charlie. It's not my real name but it's what I like to be known as."

"Eh...have you seen...?"

"Mr Murdoch's outside with the young girl. I've been here keeping an eye on you for the past two hours. Didn't want any bad spirits to take a hold of you and drag you off." Charlie held up a strange-looking bone wand which was topped with three white feathers. He gave it a shake and it produced a peculiar rattle. "Only had the one charm and I gave that to the girl."

"You know what's happened? The attack on our van—"

"Of course I know. I or I should say *we*, have been following you ever since you entered this cursed territory. With what we've seen we figured that you fellas could do with a hand."

"You mentioned *Jaku-Jimba*. The name's familiar but I can't place it."

Charlie spat. "He's bad. Bad to the bone. Worse than the *Kinie-Jer*. Worse than a crocodile with toothache. You can bet it be He who's caused all the trouble in these parts—the disease and the cha-os. It be He who's taken over the young Mr Turner."

"So, what the girl said…it's *true?*"

"You'd better bloody believe it," Charlie answered. "The old woman who cursed her brother was wicked through and through—one of the last remaining descendants of the *Walamaga People* I be-lieve Mr Murdoch told you about. The spirits must've been as mad as wallaby shit that day Mr Turner knocked her down. I mean of all the folk there, he went and hit the worst one possible. Not only did she belong to the Darkside of the Dreamtime, they reckon she was over a thousand years old."

"So, what do we do? And more importantly, can you get us out of here?"

"Kenny and Jacob are working on that right now. Come on, I'll introduce you."

Rubbing his neck, Booth followed Charlie out of the mine. Squinting against the bright sunlight, he saw, a short distance away, Murdoch, Angie and two other male aborigines. They appeared to be gathering small rocks and placing them in a circle some ten metres in diameter. "What are they doing?"

"They're making a *walabalu*—a magic circle. It should help us from *Jaku-Jimba.*"

Booth shook his head, still unwilling to believe any of this was happening. It was crazy, yet part of him knew that in order to retain his sanity he *had* to accept what was taking place as reality. At least he was no longer in that dreadful dream-world.

"Mr Booth," Murdoch called out. "If you're after some breakfast there's some biscuits and some canned peaches remaining."

"Is that it? I could do with something a bit more substantial," Booth replied, his stomach growling in protest.

"Jacob's got some cooked quoll bollocks and Kenny may have some bush tucker left."

"Christ!"

"I'm afraid that's all there is." Charlie held out his upturned palms in order to prove the point. "What game I've managed to bag is diseased. Even what water we've found is tainted. As I said before, this is a bad land. The sooner we confront this thing and get you folks out of here the better."

*   *   *   *

Throughout the course of the hot, dry morning and the even hotter afternoon, Booth learned from Angie that on their drive out here, her family had also encountered that old, one-eyed aborigine who, it now appeared, had malignly misdirected them—just what nefarious purpose had guided his actions was something which, in all likelihood, would remain a mystery but it had assuredly been intentional. Between further work preparing the *walabalu* and lookout duty, Murdoch had informed him that, from information obtained from the three aborigines, the aim was to lure Mikey to this spot and perform some sort of tribal exorcism; purging him of the demonic entity which had lived within him for thirteen years.

It was a highly risky procedure and there was no guarantee of success.

"Can you be sure that he…*it*…is still here?" Booth asked. He was sat on a flat boulder along with Murdoch, Angie and Charlie, watching as Kenny and Jacob added 'finishing touches' to the magic circle.

"Oh, He's here all right," Charlie answered. Like the other aborigines, he had now completed his own ritual preparations—his face decorated in white and yellow ochre swirls. He glanced skyward as though searching for a hidden meaning woven into the fabric of the clouds. "It'll soon be time to draw Him out. When that happens, we must all be inside the *walabalu*."

"Is it not possible that Mikey's turned back into his normal self?" Booth asked. "In fact, he could've turned back hours ago in which case he might have died out in the desert." Belatedly realising what he had just said, he turned to Angie. "Sorry, I didn't…"

Angie shrugged. "It's okay."

"Nah, the boy ain't dead." Charlie shook his head. "*Jaku-Jimba's* inside him. He's not going to let him go unless He's forced to. As for him turning back, I think we've gone beyond that stage. This could well be the last chance to save him."

"You don't think there's any other way?" Booth asked.

"There's always another way." Meaningfully and with a loud click, Murdoch snapped a large, pointed rifle cartridge into 'Barry'.

* * *

Booth was getting fidgety. Night was less than an hour away and with each minute, his sense of unease and foreboding grew. He stood within the circle of rocks and despite the presence of the others, he felt a great sense of soul-crippling loneliness. His academic pursuits had taken him to many remote and inhospitable regions of the Australian outback but this place was different, very different. There was a sense of alienness here; an unearthliness that disturbed him.

Murdoch stood, alert, rifle in hand, Angie at his side.

A small fire blazed in the centre of the *walabalu*, around which Kenny and Jacob were sat down, cross-legged. Each held an ornately carved and painted didgeridoo.

"Are you ready, Mr Booth?" asked Charlie.

"Let's get this over with."

Charlie nodded. From his belt, he removed a bladed slat of wood attached to a long cord—a bullroarer. Gesturing Booth to stand clear, he then began to spin it around his head, like a cowboy with a lasso; the fast, whirling motion creating a vibrating, roaring noise. By changing the direction and speed of the rotation, he was able to skilfully moderate the sound.

A mystical, haunting, spine-tingling drone emanated from the didgeridoos.

The sun was now a flaming orb of deep crimson that hung in the sky. Above the rugged line of the land, the sky was now a clash of vibrant red, orange and purple colours, as though the heavens had been sliced open, spilling blood and their chaotic insides.

Nervously, Booth looked in every direction, dreading what he might see. He looked up to the entrance of the abandoned mine, then back towards where the trail lay. Nothing. Was it hoping too much that this *was* just a load of fantastical nonsense and that there was nothing supernatural out there? His hope was instantly dashed on hearing a cry from Murdoch.

"Here it comes!"

Booth turned.

The ritual music ceased.

A small black whirlwind was scudding over the ground towards them at an incredible speed, throwing up a dark cloud, splintering rocks and whipping up sand. Occasionally it would jettison a shower of debris or what could have been a mangled and half-eaten small creature. Upon reaching the outer edge of the stone circle, it slowed down.

"Shoot it! For Christ's sake, shoot it!" Booth screamed.

Murdoch stood, looking down the sight of his rifle, finger on the trigger.

The darkness vanished.

At the edge of the *walabalu*, looking confused, was a naked, dark-haired, thirteen-year-old boy.

"Mikey!" Angie shouted. She rushed forward.

"*No!*" Charlie yelled. He made a grab for the girl but missed.

"You're going to be—" Angie stumbled, tripped over one of the circumference stones, dislodged it, and fell at her brother's feet.

What happened next was something that Booth could barely believe. Before his eyes, the young boy suddenly metamorphosed into a black, snarling abomination; half-man, half-Tasmanian Devil—a ghastly, therianthropic monstrosity. It stood upright, taller than an average man.

With a bloodcurdling scream, it opened its immense, fang-filled mouth, spread its claws wide and made to take a chunk out of Angie.

Murdoch fired. His aim was good, and the bullet blasted a hole in the horror's chest, throwing it back. He fired again and again, both shots finding their target, hurling the creature back further. He advanced, raised his rifle and was about to shoot a fourth time when Charlie grabbed him by the shoulder.

"We're not here to kill it!" the aborigine shouted. "We can still—"

Before any in the group could react, the injured thing assumed its dark vortex form. Like a devilish spinning top, it breached the *walabalu* at the point where it had been broken and, in its berserk fury, wrought a terrible carnage upon those inside.

Murdoch was hit full-on, his body raised off the ground and brutally torn to pieces. In a spray of gore, as though he had just walked into a large operating buzz saw, his head spiralled in one direction and a severed arm went another. The rest of him vanished; devoured almost instantaneously by *Jaku-Jimba*.

Chaos erupted.

With spears, the three aborigines stabbed at the demonic cyclone.

Jacob's weapon was dragged from his grasp, disappearing entirely. A fur-covered arm shot out from the whirling column and grabbed him, hauling him inside. His legs kicked briefly…and then he was gone, consumed by darkness.

Buffeted violently to one side, Booth tripped over Murdoch's head. He looked down. Glazed eyes stared up at him from a deeply tanned face. The lips were drawn back tightly over the white teeth in a hideous rictus of death—a sudden, violent, unexpected death.

"It's weakening!" Charlie shouted. Agilely, he rolled to one side. Snatching up a flaming branch from the fire, he sprang to his feet and drove it into the fiendish mass.

The thing howled.

The core of the vortex blazed as it became a gyrating firestorm. Wreathed in flames, *Jaku-Jimba* spun out of control. Striking the inner edge of the stone circle, it rebounded, unable to cross over.

Booth leapt out of the *walabalu*, Charlie and Kenny doing likewise.

Charlie placed the rock dislodged by Angie back in place. "We've trapped it!" he shouted triumphantly.

Over the course of the next ten minutes, Booth watched, wide-eyed, as the terrible entity became slower and slower. It was akin to a caged animal frantically seeking release but in this case, he felt no pity. Even if this thing had once been a young boy, death was now the only fate it deserved. The whirlwind died down then vanished. In its place was the hideous aberration and now that he could observe it without fearing for his life, he was reminded of *Taz*—the cartoon Tasmanian Devil. The similarities were remarkable.

Panting, tongue lolling, badly burnt and with blood streaming from numerous bullet and spear wounds, *Jaku-Jimba*—the Dreamtime demon conjured by an old aborigine witch to possess young Mikey Turner—gave a soul-shattering scream and finally fell.

* * * *

"Strange thing is you don't get any 'devils' in Australia anymore." It was the next day and Charlie sat atop a rock, gazing pensively out across the vastness of desert. "Used to, thousands of years ago. Makes me think that maybe that old witch was older than we thought."

"I'm now prepared to believe anything," Booth replied. He was hungry, thirsty and very tired.

"Anyway, I guess you and the young girl want to go home."

Booth nodded wearily. He had kept an eye on the trail that wound through this barren landscape since late yesterday and seen no traffic whatsoever, leading him to the conclusion that he was now in a realm detached from reality, void of the trappings of modern life. This belief was substantiated by all that he had witnessed over the last two days.

"And there was me beginning to think that you liked it out here." Charlie grinned. "Anyway, maybe it is time for you to leave. You modern folk don't belong in the bush."

There was a part of Booth that was expecting the aborigine to perform some kind of Dreamtime magic—to do a ritual dance and conjure forth a doorway leading to Main Street, Perth. Instead, Charlie waved a hand to Kenny who immediately got a fire going.

Black smoke drifted lazily into the azure sky.

"It's Tuesday, isn't it?" Charlie asked. "Your lift will be along soon."

* * * *

Three hours later, Booth was sat alongside 'Champ' Wrigley—the Flying Doctor from Warburton—with Angie crammed into the space behind him. Far below, like the surface of Mars, stretched the seemingly boundless Australian outback—a landscape he had once considered both awesome and beautiful but one that he now feared and abhorred. The constant hum from the propellers of the *Nomad* light aircraft were proving soporific and he found his mind drifting.

They were twenty minutes into the flight.

"That's some story, Mr Booth," Wrigley said. He was a middle-aged, bespectacled man, kind of temperament and devoted to caring for others. "But I can see you're tired. Best if you caught up on some sleep."

"I…might just…do that." Head leant against the window, Booth closed his eyes.

The plane dropped, juddering violently.

Groggily, Booth sprang awake. The first thing that struck him was how dark it was outside. Had they flown into a thunder cloud? And how long had he been asleep? Had he even been asleep? With a yawn, he turned to the pilot…and screamed.

The hirsute, one-eyed aborigine behind the controls began to laugh.

Four

The Nightmare from the Swamp

Igor Vhirinovsky cursed savagely and ran a hand down his unshaven chin. A heavy rain shower had just passed, and his murky surroundings were dismal shades of grey and green. "Aren't they ever going to stop? Just what the hell is it all in aid of?" He stood just inside the opening of a crudely built hut, dampness glinting wetly on his harshly chiselled, hit-man's features. In this godforsaken place, somewhere on the West Siberian Plain, deep within the taiga, he found himself sweating and cursing as incessantly as the thudding of the drums of the nomadic Lyushukan people—an offshoot of the better-known Ket. It was stiflingly humid and airless, yet he knew that, once the brief summer was over, this place would become a glacial, frozen land. He glared past the figure of his companion, at the village itself. It was compact and small, necessarily so, because of its impermanence. At times, the floodwaters of the fast-flowing river came rushing over its banks, prompting a move to higher ground.

"Who knows? One of their dammed rituals, probably," muttered Vyacheslav Blokhin. He took his cigar from his mouth and blew out a cloud of strong-smelling smoke. He was an ex-mercenary turned treasure hunter; a big, balding man with broad, fleshy features. "I was in Mozambique two years ago and I'm not kidding you, the drumming went on for a whole month. It was worse than the flies. Drove some of the guys I was with to the brink of madness. That was one hellish expedition, I can tell you."

"What happened?"

"Lots of things. Things I'd rather not talk about."

"As you wish." Vhirinovsky's steely eyes narrowed, taking in the preparations the tribal shamans, in their hideous furry headdresses, were engaged in; cleansing the central area with a peculiar ritual known only to themselves. He swore angrily to himself. All this would no doubt mean more delay, more frustration. For days now, it had been like this, while they waited impatiently for a guide to take them up-river, deeper into the fetid, taiga swamplands. He swore again, louder this time.

"I can't stand this constant waiting," complained Blokhin. A red blaze of anger flared up inside him. "Have you any idea how much longer?"

Vhirinovsky shook his head. There was a certain hardness about him that was like steel below the surface. He was the kind of man who needed little reason to commit murder and had indeed done so in the past. An ex-Red Army general, as a young man he had served under Khrushchev at Stalingrad, but years of disillusionment had burned the patriotism from his heart. These days his motives were purely self-serving. During his military career he had heard rumours, provided largely by the Siberian forces, who talked in hushed voices of a forgotten ruin alleged to contain tremendous wealth.

"To hell with this! There's a treasure somewhere out there that will set us up for life and knowing that we're now within spitting distance of it is driving me crazy," Blokhin vented his frustration.

"Then what do you suggest we do about it?" Vhirinovsky was deliberately sarcastic. "They won't stop the ritual just for us you know and venturing into the interior without someone who knows the way would be suicide. Men have tried in the past. None have ever returned."

Blokhin scowled and threw away his cigar butt. Deep inside, he knew that what the other said was true. The nomads were a superstitious lot. For them, the supernatural was just another facet of reality. It was something that not only existed among the darkness of the crowding trees, just over the spilling torrent of the river but which dwelt among them. All around them, every day, lurking darkly in the night.

Their journey here had been long and arduous. By rail, by car and by foot they had made their way from Omsk, crossing some truly desolate and lawless parts of Russia. Into this vast, unfriendly wilderness, in which only the hardiest of people eked out an existence, they had ventured, following in the footsteps of previous doomed expeditions in search of a legendary secret treasure.

Like an annoyed bear, Vhirinovsky throatily grumbled his frustration and impatience. The presence of something far detached from the sane world he knew was beginning to get at him now. He tried desperately to relax his mind as well as body. Here, in the stinking waterlogged forest, several hundred miles from anything that remotely resembled civilisation, it was impossible. The dark, evil forces were always present, tangible almost. Only the very foolish, or the very brave dismissed them as mere fantasies.

Suddenly, the drumming ceased.

The village became strangely silent. There was only the heavy liquid gurgle of the water in the distance beyond the fringe of pines and larches and the eerie sound of the wind over the marsh.

If only there wasn't the damp—and the eternal stench of rotting, half-decayed weeds in the river. It was too still, unnaturally so. From somewhere, an animal screamed; a harsh, thin shrill of bestial rage.

Vhirinovsky grabbed his Kalashnikov assault rifle from where it stood, propped ready against the wall of the hut. "I can't take any more of this. It's time we made a move. Come on, let's find out just what the hell's going on."

Blokhin reached for his own rifle, checking it with a smooth automatic movement, his face tight. "Have you any idea what's going to happen to us if we haven't got these negotiations figured out right?" he asked.

"What do you mean?"

"Well, what if they decide to turn against us?" Blokhin swatted a mosquito that had landed on the nape of his neck.

"Then it will just be too bad for them," answered Vhirinovsky with a savage grin, a mere skinning of his teeth. He patted his rifle meaningfully. "You should know me by now. I've got no compunction about killing anyone that gets in my way."

Together, they walked purposefully between the squat shapes of the ramshackle huts and crude tents. Step by step, not looking round, with the eyes of the hidden villagers on them, they trudged across the muddy opening. An evil-smelling wind sighed in the mournful trees, rustling the branches ominously.

The chief's hut stood in the centre of the village, slightly larger than the rest, as befitting his position. From a wolf hide-covered throne bedecked with furs, bear pelts and other forms of exotica, the hut's sole occupant, an ancient, wizened being, watched their steady approach with a sly gleam in his dark eyes. His long, tangled grey hair was draped over his knees.

"Chief Kazlak," Vhirinovsky began. "I would see the man who is to act as our guide on the journey through the swamplands. It is important that we begin as soon as possible. You know as well as I how treacherous and inhospitable this place will become if we delay too long." With an effort, he kept all trace of impatience out of his tone.

Kazlak regarded him wearily. "There will be no guide."

Vhirinovsky felt a sick feeling inside him. Days of promises and now this...His grip on the rifle tightened. He decided to try bluff as a sudden idea came to him, one that he was sure would have the desired effect and one which he cursed himself for not having thought of before. "You *will* provide us with a guide, or you will regret your rash words. We do not wish to cause trouble, but if that's the way you want it—" He left the remainder of his sentence unsaid, but his unspoken words hung quivering in the taut silence.

Kazlak's eyes narrowed. And there was a cold and emotionless look about those inhuman eyes; strange eyes, black and unblinking, filled with an empty gaze that was difficult to meet directly.

A group of villagers entered the hut, forming a ring around them, muttering to themselves, encompassing them in a large circle. Sharp-bladed knives could be seen in the hands of some.

Vhirinovsky was worried. If the worst came to the worst, he and Blokhin could no doubt kill Kazlak but that would be scant comfort when they turned and found themselves facing an angry horde of murderous, vengeful nomads.

"You say you want to go south, upriver, deeper into the swamp, towards the Hidden Lands?" asked Kazlak solemnly. He nodded his head slightly. "It is an evil place you wish to visit. A cursed place. A land of evil spirits. Why do you wish to go there?"

The air was thick with tension.

Vhirinovsky felt his throat suddenly dry. He moistened his lips nervously with a quick movement of his tongue. His mind was ticking over madly. He thought fast. It would be foolish to tell the real reason. No, this was a time for lying. "We are environmental agents of the USSR. It is our duty to prospect for new sources of natural gas, raw materials and as yet undiscovered areas of geological importance. Failure to comply with our demands will result in the forced upheaval of your people."

Kazlak uttered a harsh laugh that wobbled through his emaciated body. "You think that won't happen anyway? Moscow has already forced out many of our tribes. It will do them no good, and you are fools if you go there. You will never return. Not even your bones will be found."

Vhirinovsky straightened his back and squared his shoulders. "We will return," he said tightly. "But first we need a guide who knows the trails through the marsh. As I've already told you, we can pay well for your services."

"I would like to help you," mumbled Kazlak, shuffling his skeletal frame into a more comfortable position on his throne. "But none of my men will go into the Hidden Lands."

"What are they afraid of?" asked Blokhin uneasily.

The old chief waved a scrawny hand and one of the shamans hurried over. After a few moments of whispered conversation in their own dialect, Kazlak nodded and, arthritically, rose to his feet. "The inhabitants of the Hidden Lands are not like you or me. They are an ancient people who care and know nothing of the outside world. My people have never seen them though they are known in our myths. They live in a world of nightmare."

Vhirinovsky hesitated. *A world of nightmare!* Several times, that phrase had cropped up during his travels. Even now, he didn't know what to make of it. A chill fear coursed through his veins. Angrily, he threw it off. He smiled but there was no humour in his face. "We're afraid of no stupid superstition," he said finally, wiping a thick sheen of grime from his forehead. That was the way to look at it. Once these folk thought you were afraid, that was the end.

"Tell them," interrupted Blokhin suddenly, "that every man who goes will receive payment enough to last him for many days. They will be well recompensed by the state if any significant discoveries are made. In my short time here, I've noticed that none of your men have access to a gun...this can be remedied upon our return."

Kazlak's eyes gleamed at that. "I will tell them," he promised. "Now leave while I talk to my people. I will reach a decision come first light tomorrow."

Vhirinovsky bowed his head a little. Gripping his companion by the arm, he steered him outside. Once clear of the hut, he turned round, a savageness in his eyes. "What makes you think we can afford to give away rifles, just like that?"

"What makes you think we're ever going to come back here?" countered Blokhin, an evil glint in his eyes. "Once we get our hands on the treasure, we'll kill the guide and bypass this place. All we need to discover is how to get to these so-called Hidden Lands."

"Fair enough." Vhirinovsky nodded to himself. Of one thing he was sure. He would be watching Blokhin during the days that were to come, otherwise, he wouldn't be coming back either. There was no way of telling how the sudden possession of so much wealth would affect a man. Perhaps Blokhin himself could be conveniently removed. It would be so easy in the trackless wilds. A hundred different ways in which a man could die. Quickly, or extremely slowly, so that he screamed and pleaded for death. He pushed the dark thought away into the background of his mind. There would be time enough to think about that when a suitable opportunity presented itself.

Slowly, they moved through the village, heading back to their allocated hut.

All was quiet. There was no one else to be seen.

Vhirinovsky watched Blokhin out of the corner of his eye, walking silently beside him. Something was troubling the other. He could tell that at once. Blokhin had his head cocked a little to one side, as if listening for something—or *to* something that was almost out of earshot. He opened his mouth to speak but, with an abrupt movement, the other suddenly darted inside the shadowy opening of one of the smaller huts. For an instant, Vhirinovsky thought he heard a dull murmuring, a dry voice intoning words and phrases that were meaningless. A strange chanting, mumbled in a peculiar monotone that sent the blood racing through his veins though he didn't know why.

Then Blokhin was crying out. "So, it *was* you! I thought so. Well, this is the last time you'll work your spells on me."

Something thudded dully inside the hut. An ugly, horrible sound that was repeated twice. After that, there was a long pause.

Then Blokhin staggered out of the opening, his eyes bright. He held his rifle limply in his right hand, and there was a dark staining of blood on the heavy wooden butt. "She won't cast her damned curses on me anymore," he said shakily, his voice a racking gasp.

"What do you mean?" Vhirinovsky asked worriedly.

"I mean I just killed the old witch. What do you think I mean?"

Vhirinovsky threw a swift glance into the dimness of the hut. At first, he could see nothing. Then, he managed to make out the still figure of an old woman, lying face down on the floor. Her arms and legs were twisted beneath her body. Blood leaked from her battered head, pooling on the coarse timbers.

A single glance was sufficient to tell Vhirinovsky that she was quite dead. "You bloody fool, Blokhin! Why the hell did you have to do that?" He choked the words out as if they made a bitter taste in his mouth. His lips twisted. He glanced nervously around, hoping no one had seen his companion enter the hut.

Blokhin held out something. "It's only due to my experiences in Africa that I knew what she was up to. See what she had. Go on, take a good look for yourself." There was a rising note of hysteria in his tone. "That pain in my chest I felt the other night. I knew it wasn't a normal feeling. This old hag has been watching us ever since we arrived."

Then, all thought of what had happened fled from Vhirinovsky's mind as he saw what it was the other was holding in his hand. A crude figure of twigs and rags—a primitive doll in the image of Blokhin.

"Damned magic," said Blokhin thinly. He seemed to have a little difficulty in speaking. "I had an idea she might have been the one who was doing it."

"But why? Surely, she had no reason to—"

"Perhaps she had every reason," muttered Blokhin. He threw the figurine into the bushes. "You see, she wasn't of this tribe. I spotted that almost as soon as we entered this village. My guess is that she originally came from somewhere further south, deeper in the interior, from these so-called Hidden Lands And if she had some awareness of what we're looking for, isn't it just feasible that she would do her utmost to stop us?"

"Maybe you're right." Vhirinovsky felt his brain reel under the sudden impact of the knowledge. It had never entered his mind that their mission might be known. That made things more awkward. They would have to be on the lookout for similar devilry every single minute from now on. He threw another quick glance at the dead woman sprawled on the floor of the hut, her upturned face seemingly grinning in an unsettling, sardonic manner. Was it just his imagination or was there an expression of malicious amusement on her face, even in death? He shuddered. "We can't just leave her lying here. We're going to have to hide the body."

"As you wish," agreed Blokhin. He crouched down and got his arms under her, lifting her up.

There was an odd, strained grin on Vhirinovsky's face. "Still, you didn't have to kill her. These damned villagers won't move if they sense there's a curse hanging over either one of us. You know what they're like."

"Providing we hide the body well, they'll never know." With a grunt, Blokhin hefted the dead woman over his shoulder. "We'll take her outside and throw her in the swamp," he said grimly.

* * * *

Mile upon mile of seemingly endless marsh, broken only by stretches of half-submerged forest lay before them; several thousand square miles of unexplored, trackless quagmire. The taiga was an inhospitable wilderness through which they wound their lugubrious way slowly and arduously, their eyes wary and restless in their heads.

Vhirinovsky's hands strayed nervously towards the rifle slung over his shoulder. He marched wearily, listlessly.

Chief Kazlak had been as good as his word. A guide had been provided for them, Ychev, who knew a little true Russian. Vhirinovsky could see the other's tall, muscular figure striding ahead, hacking his way through the tall reeds that barred their way.

The terrain grew wilder and more impenetrable as they progressed, cutting and wading their way through the unforgiving wilderness.

Poisonous, choking mists from the deadly swamps curled like an impenetrable wall between them and the invisible horizon. It was agony to drag oneself along, but they did, step by step, mile by painful mile, fumbling over creepers that clutched upwards with writhing coils, and other things that slithered away with a warning hiss.

On the morning of the sixth day, the drums started again. But this time, there was something different about them. A menacing, blood-curdling undertone of insidious warning that sent dread washing strongly over Vhirinovsky's mind. Fear seared through him—a stark, unreasoning terror that was like a physical thing, lancing into his brain. He lurched into the sticky mud of the swamp that lay a couple of feet on either side of the narrow trail. There was a moment of sheer blinding panic in his brain. Then his foot came free with an ugly, squelching sound. He turned to speak to Blokhin, then stopped as Ychev came towards them.

"We must proceed with caution. We now stand at the edge of the Hidden Lands."

"Do you think we've been spotted?" asked Blokhin. His eyes flickered to the trees and the dense undergrowth, the swamp around them. He knew that at any moment their surroundings could suddenly swell full of death.

"It's possible," muttered Ychev. "They're all around us at this very moment."

"I don't see them," muttered Vhirinovsky in a quiet whisper.

"They are there." There was a note of finality in Ychev's voice.

Vhirinovsky nodded. He hefted his rifle into his right hand. There was fear in the pit of his stomach, but it was beginning to abate slightly. After all, whoever these people were, they could die just as other men. And he knew that they wouldn't have access to the kind of firepower he and his companion were carrying.

"What do you suggest?" inquired Blokhin, his eyes wide and staring.

"We keep going," said Vhirinovsky sharply. "They don't seem to be either suspicious—or particularly hostile. Probably they're just curious. Could be they've never seen outsiders before which is why they've made no move to attack us on the way in."

A few moments later, they reached a clearing in the swamp, a vast area that had been gouged out of the dense undergrowth, filled with huts fashioned from reeds.

The swamp-dwellers were gathered all around them in a vast semi-circle, waiting.

Vhirinovsky ran his judgemental gaze over them uneasily. There must have been two hundred or so of them; men, women and children—far more than he had expected from the size of the village. Their swarthy skins were painted with white and red tribal markings and many of them had applied powder and pigments to their faces in order to give them a somewhat ghoulish, skull-like appearance. There was a blankness; an emptiness to their eyes that he found deeply unsettling. He had expected them to be curious or even overtly hostile but this vacant staring was somehow worse. Much worse. It was as though they were regarding him and his expedition members as nothing more than meat.

"Looks as though we were expected," hissed Blokhin, walking warily forward. "I guess that's the chief, over by the central hut." He inclined his head slightly. "They seem friendly enough."

"*Friendly?* You've got to be kidding." Vhirinovsky looked to Ychev. "What do you think?" he asked quietly. "Think they mean trouble?"

The guide shrugged uncertainly.

Vhirinovsky waited tensely. There was a threatening tension in the air that he could almost feel, touching subtly at his nerves. He stood very still, fighting within himself to keep the expression of uneasiness from his face. Most of the natives were armed with short, stabbing spears. *How the hell could Blokhin consider them friendly?* He knew they were helpless here, utterly outnumbered. If they miscalculated, played their hand too quickly, or rashly, they would pay the price of their foolishness. He didn't know whether this tribe was cannibalistic but—

The skin covering of one of the huts was thrown aside with a suddenness that was almost numbing. Someone—something—came leaping into the centre of the clearing. A weird figure, small and hideously grotesque, the face hidden behind a death-mask, draped with the bones of slain enemies, and festooned with coloured feathers and pointed, yellow fangs.

Wicked little eyes glared at them with a red malevolence from behind tiny slits in the mask. It was obviously the shaman of the tribe. A sudden chill swept through Vhirinovsky's body. For a single, horrible moment, there seemed something familiar about the shrunken creature. His finger tightened on the trigger of his rifle. The death mask was suddenly thrown aside. He saw the other's face for the first time. Lined and wrinkled and—

It was the face of the woman Blokhin had killed back at Chief Kazak's village!

Vhirinovsky recoiled. The whole clearing was spinning and swaying insanely and there was a shrill, high laughter sounding in the air above his head. His brain shrieked at him amid the bubbling sounds. The circle of natives began moving slowly forward, pressing quietly around them. With a piercing cry, he opened fire, gunning four down in a vicious spray of bullets. Had he been thinking straight he could well have held his ground and blasted them away before they got near but instead, he spun on his heel, and raced madly away, only vaguely aware that Blokhin was behind him. Close on his heels, was the huge shape of Ychev. The roar of the villagers was becoming louder now. Then there were knives flashing in the watery sunlight and the swish of spears arcing through the air.

A war whoop sent a tingle of fear along Vhirinovsky's nerves. Something hummed over his shoulder like a flash of frozen flame. A spear stuck quivering in the tough bark of a tall tree a foot above his head. Then there was the cold bite of a knife against his arm and the warm slickness of blood flowing over his wrist. He pitched himself forward, crashing into the trees and fallen branches, climbing up, and racing on.

The trees thinned.

There was firmer ground under Vhirinovsky's running feet and he was outdistancing the bloodthirsty horde. He was out in the open, and darkness was coming up out of the far horizon, and there were tall trees in front of him. Uttering a barrage of expletives, Blokhin came splashing towards him, Ychev at his heels.

There was a pause in the wild shouting behind them.

"We've given them the slip," gasped Vhirinovsky. He forced himself to breathe quietly. Gradually, the mad hammering of his heart lessened and slowed to a more normal pace.

"It's not that," Ychev panted. "They won't come any further."

"Why not?" asked Blokhin, looking back to ensure they weren't being followed. Blood trickled down his face from where he had run into a branch. He had lost his rifle.

There was a curious expression on Ychev's face. He was silent for a moment. Then, with a shaking hand he pointed before him. "Look!"

Vhirinovsky and Blokhin turned to follow his pointing finger.

From out of the swamp rose a huge mound of hardened earth ringed with a copse of hideous, straggling trees. Atop the hill was a ghastly structure. It was a ramshackle hut festooned with weeds in which could be seen the discoloured bones of the dead. Stakes had been driven into the ground each one surmounted by a rotting head. Posts carved with eldritch sigils leant at strange angles and large, bat-winged creatures flew around them.

A foul stench polluted the air.

"The legends are true!" cried Ychev. "The house of Baba Yaga!"

"There's no such being," snapped Vhirinovsky. "She doesn't exist. It's just some stupid superstition, invented to keep thieves away. An old legend, handed down over the centuries." He glanced back, ensuring none of the villagers were approaching. "Still no sign of them," he said with a nod of satisfaction.

Blokhin twisted his head and looked about him. There was a menace in the silence that clung about them, squeezing itself around them with hidden, sadistic fingers. "Let's hope the legends are true regarding the treasure. If so, it will be up there somewhere. Come on, let's move!"

Ychev was too frightened to go up so they left him on watch at the base of the mound informing him to holler a warning at the first sign of trouble.

The very soil, silt and mud of which the mound was formed seemed infected with evil, as though it possessed a malign, mischievous force which seemed to trip, cling and sink with every boot which fell on it. Filthy water, laced with what looked like blood, bubbled, squelched and flowed in rivulets from the befouled ground. In places, ragged skeletons protruded from the earth.

"It's one massive corpse heap," said Blokhin, staring at the ground with disgust. "A midden filled with the dead. And that stink. It's horrendous."

Fighting back his revulsion, Vhirinovsky ploughed on, focusing on the wicked looking structure at the summit. The terrible, corpse-saturated mud was now up to his knees.

As they struggled higher, they could see that there were numerous sinkhole-like openings here, dark cavernous mouths that gaped out of the slope like soulless eyes, black and empty.

Vhirinovsky shivered despite the tight hold he had on himself, fighting against the growing feeling that there were things inside this cursed barrow. Dim, vague things, that were evil. Made and born of that same horror that had fashioned the unbelievable nightmare back in the village. His grip on his rifle tightened.

A noisome green mist began to rise from the ground.

Suddenly the earth beneath them subsided and they found themselves sinking deep as, with a loud slurping sound, they were sucked down. One moment they were up to their waists, then their chests until, within a matter of seconds, they were pulled under completely. Panic and horror threatened to overcome them as everything darkened and breathing became impossible. The nightmare went on for the best part of a minute until, accompanied by a ghastly assemblage of bones, they splashed down into a huge, subterranean pool of rank water.

Surfacing, Vhirinovsky took a deep breath and swam to one side, pulling himself free of the underground pond. He heard splashing and cursing and then Blokhin emerged.

It was pitch dark.

Vhirinovsky unslung his pack and rummaged around for his torch. Switching it on he was surprised to see the hewn stone walls of the huge chamber they were in. Wiping away the worst of the mud, he panned the torch over the water, seeing if he could find his rifle which he had dropped on his passing through the ground and into this stygian hell.

"Where the hell are we?" asked Blokhin, looking around incredulously.

"I've no idea. I'd guess this place must be a thousand years old. Maybe older." Vhirinovsky was scared although he tried not to show it. "Come on, we have to get out of here. Let's see if we can find a way up. He started for a shadowy opening visible at the extremity of his torchlight.

To their dismay they found that the passage beyond sloped down.

Darkness fell around Vhirinovsky like some evil, ominous cloak. The ground was smooth beneath his boots, dipping downwards and away into a black nothingness. The walls dripped moisture and somewhere there was the dull splash of something slithering away.

He swung the beam around in a wide, sweeping arc. Black shadows scurried away into corners of ebon silence.

Slowly, they inched their way along. It was difficult to keep upright and at the same time to keep their hands sliding along the wall because the floor of the cave was slipping and sloping away from them.

Vhirinovsky began to feel physically sick, the light from his torch chasing the little midnight shadows momentarily out of his path. But always, they came back and closed in behind them as they progressed. Like an endless wall of blackness that stretched for an indeterminate distance before and behind them.

"How much further does this go?" Blokhin's voice was a floating murmur.

"No idea."

Blokhin snorted at that but said nothing.

"The treasure must be down here somewhere. This has to be the place. A ruined temple perhaps..." Vhirinovsky pulled his body forward. There was an outjutting corner of stone in front of him. He rounded it with an effort, then stopped. Glancing down, he found emptiness beneath him; black and awful. A seemingly bottomless abyss. For a mad moment, he teetered on the brink, straining desperately to maintain his balance. In his mind's eye, he could visualise himself falling through that blackness, down, down, down—dying of dehydration before he struck the bottom. Then, abruptly, the vertigo passed. He swallowed and looked across at Blokhin. The other's face was a dim white blur in the torchlight. And there was a faint gleam of fear in his eyes, but it faded almost at once.

"I wonder how deep it is." Blokhin picked up a small rock from the ground at his feet and dropped it over the side.

For long moments, they could hear it, crashing against the sides of the pit with a hollow, wailing clatter that was horrible to hear. Slowly, it drifted away to the edge of silence, then stopped altogether. After that, there was nothing.

"Hell!" muttered Blokhin. He swayed back. "It goes down a long way." Fear edged his voice, showed once more in the half-shadow of his face.

With a conscious physical effort, Vhirinovsky forced steadiness into the muscles of his arm, and shone the torch over the edge. For an instant, he could see nothing. Then, gradually, he was able to make out details.

Below the jagged lip of the pit, some thirty feet down, another cave showed vaguely as a dark opening, a gaping mouth in the side. There was a narrow ledge of rock below it.

Blokhin had seen it too. He pointed a shaking finger. "Looks as though there's something down there," he said sharply, wincing a little as the distant walls flung back faint echoes of his words.

"Think we could reach it with the rope?" asked Vhirinovsky.

"You're determined to go down there, then?"

"Of course. Do you know any other way? Maybe it'll lead to a way out."

Blokhin unstrapped his pack and took out a second torch and a coil of rope which he dropped to the rough floor, casting about for a suitable place to anchor it. Finally, he looped it over an upthrusting needle of rock, then threw the other end into the unbroken blackness of the pit.

Vhirinovsky glanced down. Nausea was strong in him now. He had no more fear of heights than any other man, but that emptiness beneath him did something to his nerves.

"I'll go first if you want," said Blokhin, slinging the torch over a shoulder. He crouched down and lowered himself over the edge.

In the torchlight, Vhirinovsky watched him go, a black, squat figure climbing down the sheer wall of the pit.

Blokhin reached the top of the narrow ledge, threw a swift glance upwards, and then vanished inside.

Vhirinovsky waited. The silence grew long, and the shadows seemed more evil and menacing, living things of the dark that almost *breathed* on his neck. Slowly, the minutes lengthened. Leaning far out, he saw the ledge. But there was no sign of his companion. The rope was still there, dangling freely against the dark. He leaned out, snatched at it wildly, feeling it suddenly rough and burning between his fingers. He caught a tight hold of the rope, feeling that awful drop beneath him, pulling subtly at his swinging body. Fastening the torch to his belt, slowly, hand over hand, he lowered himself down. Terror clutched at his brain and cut like a knife into his racing heart.

He was suddenly quite sure there was something as black as the pit and twice as awful waiting down there to strike up and tear him down, to rend him apart. But there was no way back now. He would have to go on. Even if he could talk himself into going back, he doubted whether he had that much strength left to pull himself up again. There was a dull roaring in his ears and a peculiar tightness behind his eyes. His arms felt as if they could hold on no longer. He couldn't breathe. He was caught in some vast web of blackness, held fast, and there was no way out. It was no use screaming. He felt sure of that. Because the loudest sound in the whole of creation would be swallowed up and lost in the great void around him.

Something hard and sharp struck against his feet. He had reached the ledge. Carefully, he swung himself in. The cave was larger than he had expected, a cold chamber of chill quietude. The floor was oddly smooth, unnaturally so, and covered with something slippery that shone with a dull gleam in the light of the torch. He looked about for Blokhin. But there wasn't the slightest trace of— Something moved at the back of the cave. There was a round opening that obviously led through to another cave at the back. It filled suddenly. He swung his torch.

"Blokhin?"

Suddenly his mind was a screaming turmoil. For the first time, he saw what it was. A vast, obscene creature, forty feet or more in length; it slithered forward on its belly with a tortuous motion as if it were trying to move several times faster than a perverse nature had intended. The mouth was a nightmare slit of drooling horror. A deep triangular travesty of a mouth, rimmed with gaping, brown fangs and beslimed tusks spilled a torrent of gelatinous fluid in front of it, lubricating the rocky floor. A single red eye glared balefully from out of the centre of the great, veiny, bulbous head. It had arms—strangely human arms; massive and leprous white, at the end of which were huge taloned hands. One claw crushed Blokhin's body in its murderous grip before cramming him into its gaping maw and biting him in two, gorily gulping down the man's upper half.

Vhirinovsky's mind screamed at him.

Still, the creature came on, dragging itself like a burrowing mole on those hideously human hands. For an instant, he stood still, paralysed, rooted to the spot. Beyond the horror he could see an exit from the cave. Then something seemed to buckle inside him. With a piercing cry, he fled for the opening, leaping clear as it brought its slavering bulk towards him, reaching with one of its outstretched hands.

And then he was running as the horror slid behind him, his heart threatening to explode in his chest. Leaping over ravaged skeletons and weaving through slimy heaps of reeking excrement, he dashed into the darkness, taking small comfort in the fact that he was now going up.

From the diminishing sound he knew he was outdistancing it. Still, he ran on. For an unknown time, he made his way up until he came to a place where the way ahead was blocked by a heap of contorted skeletons. Frantically, he set about clearing the grisly obstacle, heaving the slime-covered bones to one side. Beyond, the tunnel ran for about thirty yards before reaching a dead end.

Vhirinovsky's heart sank. There was no escape.

Madly, desperately, he staggered forward, searching for a way out. He was becoming dizzy with fear and exertion. The walls were cold and damp against his palms. Something seemed to infiltrate his mind; a dark, insidious laughter the came from everywhere—yet he could see no one. And far-off, yet getting nearer, came a loathsome slurping as the nameless abomination, that thing from the subterranean depths, dragged its way towards him. As he began to pass out he thought he heard a peal of horrible laughter.

* * * *

It was all a nightmare, Vhirinovsky told himself as, accompanied with a loud hammering, he regained consciousness, the sound of Ychev shouting and beating at the wooden door of the horrendous room he was in breaking through the darkness. With a crash, the door flew open, spilling a meagre amount of grey daylight into the dismal confines. In the doorway stood the guide, his face a mask of absolute horror.

Now that Vhirinovsky could make out his surroundings better, he felt bile rise to his throat. He lay, bound with rope, in the corner of a small room that was filled with thousands of fragments of bone. Mouldy hip bones, femurs, rib cages and skulls lay scattered all over the floor. Some of the piles were knee-high in places. Bones hung from the ceiling like ghoulish ornaments. A huge black cauldron in the fireplace was crammed full of them.

The stink of the long-dead pervaded everything. It was visible as a brown mist that hovered near the raftered ceiling.

"Help me!" Vhirinovsky yelled.

Ychev cried out something in his own language before dashing over to where the other lay. He withdrew a knife and cut the thick bonds. "Come on. We must get out of here before she returns."

Massaging his wrists, Vhirinovsky got to his feet. He rushed for the door, fearing that it would suddenly slam shut, closing off that sane rectangle of daylight, plunging them both into an abysmal darkness. He reached the threshold and saw that he was at the top of the dreadful hillock. Below him, and in every direction, the swamp extended for as far as the eye could see.

Suddenly a gangrenous, clawed hand burst from the earthen floor, grabbing Ychev.

The guide screamed and frantically tried to pull away, but the grip was vice-like.

Dislodging clods of dirt, a corpse-like figure began to pull itself upright. With a supernatural strength, it tightened its hold and then twisted, snapping the unfortunate guide's leg at the shin. Ychev hollered out his agony and fell backwards, crashing into a heap of skulls.

With an obscene gargling laugh, the horror emerged fully from the grave-like pit. It was a hideously shrivelled and emaciated entity. Stained and torn linen and fur garments were wound around much of the ghoul, but the exposed parts were brownish-green revealing glimpses of leather-hardened, desiccated skin. Bone amulets and tarnished bracelets had been incorporated into its wrappings. Its face was stretched, the skin lumpy and mottled. Tufts of black, ragged hair sprouted from its head and lambent red fires burned in the depths of its otherwise empty eye sockets.

Although the guide had risked his life to save Vhirinovsky, he felt no obligation to reciprocate. Instead, he turned and fled, bounding down the slope, plunging through the deep sludge in which the dead festered. Streaked with mud, he was now laughing insanely. Tripping, he fell face first into the morass.

There came a loud creaking, slurping sound from behind.

Terrified, he turned to look over his shoulder and what he saw finally broke his mind.

The strange, weed-festooned hut was rising from the ground!

On a pair of long and spindly, reptilian legs, akin almost to those of a giant chicken, the structure rose fifteen feet into the air. In the open doorway was the cadaverous witch, hurling her curses. The bizarre construction started down the slope towards Vhirinovsky.

In a few lurching strides it overtook the doomed man, and he felt the large, splayed foot push him to the sodden ground where the foul swamp mud suffocated him as he struggled helplessly. The last sensation he knew was the agony of his spine breaking.

* * * *

Some indeterminable time later, Vhirinovsky opened his eyes. He could see the anaemic sun beginning to rise beyond the horrible swamp. He had made it! Somehow, he must have escaped. Then he noticed that he was some distance off the ground and could not feel his legs, in fact, he realised he could feel nothing below his neck. There was a groaning noise to his right and he swivelled his eyes in that direction. The bloody head of Ychev had been placed on a stake and he saw the head's eyes begin to open. Frantically looking around him, Vhirinovsky finally understood the dreadful truth.

The screaming of the severed, but alive, heads tore through the forest as the sun rose over the Hidden Lands.

Five

The Black Spirit Storm

The stark and glacial wilderness of the Canadian Northwest Territories surrounded the isolated geological research station. Here, close to the Yukon border, the glaring whiteness of snow covered the Mackenzie Mountain trails and swept down in a single stretch of eye searing white to the pine tree-covered valley almost two thousand feet below.

Professor Alexander Moorcroft stared out into the far distance, his ruddy features displaying frustrated annoyance. This was supposed to be a flying visit, and he had urgent business back in Toronto in a few days which he could not afford to miss. This was only the second time he had been here and the prospect of being stranded for the foreseeable future irked him considerably. "You say there's absolutely no chance of getting down to the valley at all today? You're quite sure?"

"I'm saying it would be extremely difficult, if not impossible." Chogan, the Native American engineer and expert on the local area, nodded his greying head emphatically and spread his hands out wide in a gesture of apology. "It is far from usual to get such heavy snow cover at this time of year."

"It appears that we're stuck here, professor," said Doctor Ronald Chalmers, the team leader and the man responsible for the day-to-day running of the station. His face was furrowed into a tightly controlled mask of impatience. "News is that there has been a fresh fall of snow this side of the Wrigley Pass. Most of the trail leading to the valley has been completely snowed under and there are warnings of further falls."

"I see." Moorcroft walked away from the window and lowered himself into a nearby chair. "And until it clears, we're confined here." He had arrived the night before and taken little more than a passing interest in the research team, intending to leave the next day with the samples he had come to collect. His gaze wandered swiftly from one to the other, taking in details with a practised eye in the realisation that he could well be cooped up with them for the foreseeable future. Firstly, there was Chogan, small and tough, thoroughly capable and completely at home in the mountains. A reliable man to have around in a crisis like that which faced them now. Thickset, with shoulders like an ox, and square, rugged features that might almost have been chiselled out of the very rock itself. This man knew the mountains like the back of his own hand and was well acquainted with their dangers and their hidden treachery. By contrast, Chalmers was tall and fair-haired, bespectacled and in his early thirties. He had been based up here for the past three months along with his wife, Janice, who was herself a professional geologist. She was sat over to one side, busily going through some of the detailed paperwork. Two others, Sam Kuttner and Brian Munro, both research students, were elsewhere in the base.

"My guess is that it will be at least a couple of days before the way becomes passable. Perhaps more," said Chogan, noting the frustration on the professor's features.

"Christ! If I'd known it was going to be like this I wouldn't have come here." Moorcroft scowled. He hadn't prepared himself for this but perhaps he should have known better. He let out a resigned sigh. "Ah well, I suppose I've got to make the best of an unfortunate situation. It's just one of those things, I guess." Inwardly, now that the shock of impending isolation was beginning to wear off, he felt bored. There wasn't much for him to do, except sit this out and listen to the infrequent weather reports on the small radio. And they weren't very encouraging.

Chalmers threw a glance at his wife before heading over and sitting next to the clearly disgruntled professor. "Would you care for a Scotch? I'll freely confess to you that it's how most of us get through the day. When you're based up here for weeks on end, as most of us have been, you take your comforts where you can."

Moorcroft shook his head. "Not for me, thanks."

"Suit yourself." Chalmers idly picked up a magazine. "You know, one of us might manage to get down and assess things. Get a more localised view as opposed to what the regional forecast is. But I wouldn't advise anyone to be too hasty as there's another storm coming up. Mark my words, we'll be snowed under before nightfall."

* * * *

Moorcroft lay in his bed and listened to the wild fury of the wind as it howled and hammered outside. He could hear it as it shrieked around the base like a maddened beast, shaking the windows, piling the snow in great drifts against the walls. Desperately, he tried to shut out the awful, keening noise, and to make himself as comfortable as possible. There was something almost frightening about the insane violence of the storm outside.

He rolled over onto his side, closed his eyes and tried to get some sleep. But it was no use. The movement had brought him face-to-face with the window, looking out to the terrible blackness outside. Despite the overall darkness of the berserk heavens, there was sufficient moonlight for him to make out some of the surface details. In the far distance, the gigantic sweep of the nearby peaks towered high above the base, sharp pinnacles of ice and snow that seemed to point accusing fingers towards the heavens.

Fear was cold along his spine as he stared outside. It seemed relatively harmless when looked at from the comparative comfort of his small room. But was it? Could anyone be sure for certain? Could it be that there *were* things yet unknown to science and reason out there?

He was not by nature a superstitious man but even so he was afraid. It took all the mental discipline he possessed to face the madness of night that screamed outside with a bestial fury and still retain a tight hold of himself.

His thoughts stopped abruptly as he saw a bizarre shadow move past the small square window five feet away. Almost instinctively, he jerked upright, his eyes wide in his head. He tried to tell himself that it had just been the wind hurling the thick snow before it. But that wasn't the real explanation. He was sure of that.

And then he saw it again. There *was* something outside. Sudden, primitive fear came rushing, surging into his mind, lancing coldly into his brain. The age-old fear inherent in every man. The fear of the darkness—and the things that lurked therein.

Trembling, he looked about him. He moved his head very slowly, unwilling, yet unable not to look at that square of darkness; scared that at any moment he would see something terrible pressed up against the glass and that it would drive him insane.

Breathing deeply, he tried to tell himself that perhaps it was nothing more than an animal.

Above the wail of the wind, he could hear the sound of movement outside and now he was convinced that there was something there. But what? In his mind, he began to hear faint tribal singing, the kind he was familiar with having been on several Native American reservations. Yet this possessed a nightmarish, soul-wrenching quality that played havoc with the mind, conjuring up ghastly images of the dead and the diseased and the foul, half-man, half-beast creatures that fed on them, of battlefields strewn with the rotting corpses of fallen braves at which the crows pecked and ancient, withered medicine men performing unholy rituals in the solitude of their tepees. Was it just his imagination or could he now hear an unholy drumming? Desperately, he fought against the whimpering horror that threatened to overwhelm him

Curiosity battled with panic and the blind, howling terror in his mind. Forcing down the fear, he swung his legs to the cold floor and crossed over slowly towards the window.

The sound intensified, followed by a shrill caterwaul that sent tiny shivers of ice spilling up and down the muscles of his back. The hairs on his neck ruffled uncomfortably. Whatever had produced that dreadful screech certainly didn't sound like any animal he had ever heard before.

He reached the window and, mustering his courage, he put his face up to it, allowing him to make out the details beyond. Something unbelievably gaunt and tall—eight, perhaps nine feet in height—detached itself from the wall near the entrance to the base like an evil, threatening shadow gifted with movement. It moved, seemingly unimpeded, through the heavy blizzard before stopping at the main door to the base.

Moorcroft felt suddenly ill. A twin set of red, glowing eyes stared back at him. He caught a fragmentary glimpse of a hook-nosed face; grey-white and terribly wrinkled, framed by a long, ragged, black-feathered headdress, with slavering, pointed teeth in a caricature of a human mouth and rotting strips of beadwork and wampum-bedecked garments that clung grotesquely around an emaciated body. In one hand it held what looked like a tomahawk. He took a step away from the window, gasping for air, choking back the scream that rose unbidden to his lips. Then, unable to stop himself, he turned and ran shrieking out of his room.

A whirling chaos threatened to overwhelm him. That pair of lambent red eyes staring out of the ghastly corpse-face continued to burn in his mind. He fought desperately against the hideousness and the insanity that came crowding in, stumbling along the narrow passage, muttering incoherent profanities, trying to pull himself together, only vaguely aware of other doors being flung open, of light streaming brilliantly into the corridor so that it chased away the shadows. And then voices were shouting madly in his ears.

Someone seized his arm and held on tightly.

"Professor! For God's sake, pull yourself together!" Chalmers shouted. "What is it? What happened?"

Moorcroft was shaking as he allowed the other to lead him to a nearby chair in the main lounge. Gratefully, he sank down into it. A drink was hastily prepared and placed into his shaking hand.

"What's going on?" inquired Munro, buttoning up his pyjama top. He was a small, bearded man who looked constantly nervous and almost as frightened as Moorcroft himself.

"I'm all right." The professor took a sip from the whisky glass. "Nothing to panic about. I'm all right now."

"Something must have happened." Chalmers came forward, his face a mask of concern. "What was it? A nightmare?"

Moorcroft clasped his head in his hands and leaned his elbows forward on his knees. "Maybe," he said. "I don't know. Perhaps I did dream it all. Though I could have sworn there was something in the snow outside the window of my room. Something that— God! It was horrible." He shuddered.

"Well, it couldn't have been one of us," said Kuttner, the youngest of the team. He looked around, doing a quick headcount. "We're all accounted for. Besides, it's thirty below out there and with this dammed wind it's probably more like minus fifty. Nothing human could survive out there for long."

"Can you describe what you saw?" asked Chalmers.

"Only vaguely, I'm afraid. It was tall, with glowing red eyes and its face..." Moorcroft finished his drink in one gulp, wincing as the raw liquor burnt the back of his throat.

Chalmers looked doubtful. *"Red eyes? Are you sure?"*

"I don't know. Maybe I was dreaming. But it seemed so damn real."

"Well, if there is anything strange out there it had best stay outside." Chalmers disappeared into his room and came back a moment later with his rifle. "If it tries to get in, this will soon take care of it."

"If it wasn't a dream, he had then you're a fool if you think you'll be able to stop it with a gun," broke in Chogan, stepping forward and turning to Chalmers.

Moorcroft looked up. There was a tight expression on his face. "Just what do you mean by that remark?" he snapped.

Chogan began pacing the room, his face strained and hard. "Who knows?" he muttered finally. "Very few people have ever seen it face-to-face and lived to tell the tale. Yet, amongst my tribe, we have tales of the Wind-Walker."

"Come on, Chogan, spare us the superstitious nonsense," hissed Kuttner. "I've heard your stories before. The professor just had a bad dream. That's all. Besides, if we're to be stranded here for several days, the last thing we want to hear is your ghost stories. That will do nothing for our peace of mind."

"Well, I'm going to look around. Who wants to come with me?" Chalmers said, putting on his heavy fleece.

For a moment, no one replied.

It was Kuttner who eventually spoke up: "I'll go with you. Just give me a minute to get my coat."

"You're being fools, both of you," said Janice. "It's far too cold outside and you'll never find any tracks. That will have to wait until morning."

Moorcroft had to agree. It was insane to go out there on a night such as this, to hunt around for evidence of something he may, or may not, have seen. "Obviously it's up to you what you want to do, but I'm going to go back to my room." He rose from his chair and, taking his drink with him, made his way slowly along the narrow corridor towards his room and stepped inside, closing the door gently behind him. For a long moment, he stood quite still, with his back hard against the cold, solid woodwork of the door, not daring to look at the black square that marked the position of the window. Then, finally, he managed to lift his gaze.

There was nothing there. He crossed over slowly, just to make sure. But the dark shadows outside were still. All was as it should be.

The events of the past quarter of an hour had made him feel light-headed. He turned his back on the window, went to his bed and closed his eyes, finally drifting off into a troubled sleep.

* * * *

When Moorcroft awakened, it was from a ghastly nightmare in which he had been floundering desperately through knee-deep snow, pursued by ugly, screaming, whistling shapes, gruesome and distorted, that came rapidly nearer with every step.

He got up out of bed, walked across to the window and looked out.

It had stopped snowing sometime during the latter part of the night, but there were still a few dark clouds boiling threateningly above the high peaks of the surrounding mountains. He threw them an appraising glance, half-turned from the window, then stopped. He felt his stomach muscles quiver uncontrollably.

Outside, where he had thought that he had seen that creature last night, he could see Chalmers and Chogan, muffled in their heavy parka coats, scanning the ground. He could tell by the way they were looking around that they had discovered something. Fear suddenly blazed in him—stark, completely unreasoning horror that was like a mad thing in his brain.

So there had been something out there in the darkness. Something that had crept away into the shadows or had perhaps sought some other means of entering the base.

He had no time to mull these disturbing thoughts over in his mind. He lurched away from the window and hurriedly got dressed. All the time, his mind kept coming up with a multitude of burning questions that shrieked to be answered, but for which there were no answers.

Opening the bedroom door, he walked out into the corridor and entered the main room.

"Looks like you were right after all, professor," muttered Kuttner. "Chogan discovered tracks not an hour ago. Better have a look at them yourself."

Moorcroft returned to his room and got his heavy coat. He was heading back, intent on going outside when, with a blast of freezing cold air, the main door opened and Chalmers and Chogan entered, hastily closing the door behind them. There was a look of confusion imprinted on their ruddy faces.

"Seems that there *was* something outside the base last night," said Chalmers, taking off his coat.

"Any idea what it could have been?" Moorcroft asked.

"It's like nothing I've ever seen before in all my years in the mountains," Chogan said, obviously picking his words with caution. "We were hoping you might be able to help us. You claim to have seen this creature. Do you think you could describe it more accurately than you did last night?"

"Not really," replied Moorcroft. He tried to think, but it was useless. Memory seemed to reach him through a thick fog. It was as if the thing he had seen the night before had been so horrible, so utterly alien, that his mind was baulking at the attempt to recall it. Dimly, he remembered something tall and grotesque, pale and cold, like the night from which it had come with a hideous, corpse-like face. And the glowing red eyes that had looked soullessly into his own. Briefly, he told them all that he could remember.

Chogan frowned. "I see. As you said yourself, there wasn't much, but what little you've been able to tell us has convinced me that we're all in deadly danger as long as we remain here. I've heard many tales during my life in this land about the spirits—the manitous—that roam the mountain trails after dark. The worst of these is Ithaqua, the—"

"That's enough, Chogan," interrupted Chalmers. "I'll admit that those tracks out there belong to neither man nor any beast I know of in these parts but that isn't reason to suggest anything supernatural. Something had been prowling around the base last night, something that had no right to be here, but it's gone now." He looked about the worried faces of those inside. "You hear me? It's gone."

"Surely we're safe inside anyway?" said Munro, nervously.

Chalmers turned towards him. "Of course we are."

"That remains to be seen." Chogan had paced over to the large stone hearth where a welcoming fire blazed. "Personally, I think one of us should try and make our way down the pass to see how badly blocked the road is. There's just a chance that the storm may have cleared away most of the fallen snow."

"You're going to have trouble getting the snowcat down there. Besides, I've still got quite a bit of work to do repairing the treads," said Kuttner.

"I wasn't planning on taking it. I'll go down on foot," Chogan replied.

"You really don't want to stay here another night, do you?" asked Munro. Despite the fact that it was morning, he had already started on the whisky. "What exactly is it you fear, Chogan?"

"Yes, what is it?" Moorcroft asked, not knowing whether he wanted to truly know the answer. It was clearly now a fact that something terrible in appearance and perhaps in nature had been outside the base.

Chogan looked briefly at Chalmers, contemplating whether to relate what he knew. A moment past before he began to speak: "I am of the Mi'kmaq tribe, one of the Algonquian people. There is a story we tell around our campfires when the sky is dark and the wind howls from the frozen North, concerning the evil spirit, the Wendigo. Of all the manitous it is the most depraved, glorifying in acts of cannibalism and horror. It can change its shape, assume the forms of its totemic beasts, yet its true appearance is exactly as the professor described. It is said that it can possess the minds of men, drive them insane and turn them into raging, flesh-eating monsters."

"Whilst I respect your customs, Chogan, it all sounds a load of scare-mongering rubbish," said Kuttner. "No doubt there was something out there but it sure as hell wasn't a ghost or anything of that sort."

"If that's what you think, fine." Chogan shrugged his shoulders. "But I for one don't want to be here when the sun goes down."

"So, you think this thing will come back?" asked Moorcroft.

Chogan nodded. "I'm sure it will. Last night it was just scouting, assessing our defences. That's why I think it is vital that I go and see if there's a way for us to get down to the valley."

* * * *

Half an hour later, Moorcroft stood at the wide windows and watched the short, thick-set figure of the Native American making his way down the snow-covered side of the mountain.

"With any luck, he'll make it all right," said Chalmers. "Once he gets to the pass everything will be plain sailing. He's a good man and I don't think he'll be foolish enough to take any unnecessary chances. If all goes well, he should be back well before sundown. And if he does find the way is passable then all of us could be out of here before it gets dark. I know my wife would much rather be heading for Wrigley than stay cooped up here any longer than is necessary."

Moorcroft nodded. His mouth was set into a tight line across the middle of his face. Somehow, though, he didn't think things would be quite as easy as that. At the back of his mind, a little, nagging thought kept skipping into the background of his brain, refusing to come out into the open, where he could recognise it for what it actually was—but whatever it was it was laden with dread. Shading his eyes against the wicked glare of the sun that was thrown up from the vast, white expanse of snow, he caught a final dark shadow as Chogan disappeared from view.

"I take it you're not buying any of this talk about evil spirits and the like, are you?" Chalmers asked, turning to the professor.

"Me? I don't know. I've been trying to wrack my brains for other possible explanations, and I can't come up with any. However, regardless of what I think, we should play this down for the sake of the others. The last thing we need is for panic set in." Moorcroft stepped back from the window.

"Chogan has been talking about a lot of weird things while he's been up here. This isn't the first time he's mentioned this *Wendigo*. He's told me quite a bit about it."

"Given our circumstances, the less I hear about that, the better. Anyway, have you had any success in re-establishing radio contact?"

Chalmers shook his head. "Not yet, although Munro's working on it. Mountain Rescue know that we're out here, however they don't know anything of our current plight. If we're stuck here for another couple of days and we've been unable to fix the radio then I'm sure they'll send out a helicopter or a patrol just to check on us."

* * * *

When Chogan failed to return seven hours later, Moorcroft, Chalmers and Kuttner went out to search for him. They had initially set out in the hastily repaired snowcat before being forced to abandon it after finding it unable to cope with the descent.

The raging wind swooped down from the mountain peaks at their backs.

Full darkness was still somewhere far away in the frozen distance; a black, brooding thing that would come rushing up out of the sky as soon as the sun went down. And all around them, the snow, picked up by the heavy gusts, fell in blinding sheets across the face of the slope.

Despite the harsh conditions, Chalmers soon managed to pick up the guide's trail. "We'll have to hurry," he shouted as he led the way into the icy wilderness. "At a guess, I'd say there's only perhaps a couple of hours of daylight left. Maybe less." Violent gusts threatened to whip away his words.

Conversation became useless as they set off down the slope, the wind now screaming in their ears, slapping monstrously against their faces, freezing exposed flesh and chilling the blood.

Moorcroft kept his gaze straight ahead. His eyes, under the fur-lined hood of his heavy coat, were never still, watching intently for the slightest movement. But for a long while, there was nothing, only the two figures of his companions up ahead. Minutes ticked past, lengthening along with their shadows as all around them the high-pitched howling of the incessant wind blew loudly. A biting coldness ate into their bodies, numbing, stiffening their muscles. Surely, they should have found Chogan by now, he thought as he glanced around, uneasily taking in the harsh terrain. Soon it would be impossible for them to go any further.

The wind picked up in strength, becoming a full-blown blizzard, a near whiteout. Within minutes, it had closed around them. A thick, virtually impenetrable wall of swirling snowflakes; a frozen maelstrom.

For the best part of an hour, they ploughed on into the deepening snow.

In spite of the tight hold he had on himself, Moorcroft shivered and not just from the sub-zero temperature. His mind kept spewing up gruesome images of what might have happened to the Native American. He tried to stop it. But it continued, going around in circles, endlessly, and the result was just the same. Supposing, he thought, that the thing he had seen outside the base had ambushed Chogan. He shuddered. Even his usually calmly scientific mind had been seriously affected by what he had seen and by the anxiety of the past few hours. There was no denying it—this wasn't a land where men ought to be. Not out here, in the great, white spaces between the cruel mountain peaks, where the wolf-wind came howling down out of the Arctic North. A mad wind, that howled into the mind as well as eating at the body.

"*Chogan!*" Chalmers hollered. He shouted out the name twice more before turning round to the others. He briefly consulted his watch. "There's nothing more we can do. Let's return to the base before it gets dark. It's possible that he's backtracked, and we've missed him."

* * * *

For a time, Moorcroft had the dreadful, unnerving feeling that they were not going to make it to the base. A gloom had fallen and the uphill struggle, into the savage wind, tested each man's endurance to the utmost. Thus it was with a great sigh of relief that he saw the abandoned snowcat and then the welcoming lights of the research station glowing dimly through the dense blizzard that swirled all around them.

After ten more minutes, his leg muscles jolting with every step, and now that they were less than a hundred or so yards away, he crumpled to the snow with the utter exhaustion of it all. Sudden shock propelled him backwards. For there, lying face-up, half-buried before him, eyes staring sightlessly out of his face, was the body of Chogan. In one icy blue hand, grasped in a death-grip, was a strange bone amulet. The broken wooden shaft of his small ice-pick projected oddly from the frozen ground nearby.

"Christ! Wha...what—?" Kuttner choked on his words.

Moorcroft felt his legs weaken and quiver as he tried to stand up, his gaze glued to the sight before him. For one dreadful moment he was irreverently reminded of pictures he had seen of preserved mammoths exhumed from the Siberian tundra.

"We can't leave him out here," muttered Chalmers as soon as he could speak and still keep his voice steady. He bent down and with a gloved hand gingerly touched the corpse. It was frozen solid.

"It looks as though he may have suffered a heart attack," said Kuttner.

Chalmers nodded grimly. "It's hard to say. We'll have to take him back."

Even though they were so near, Moorcroft knew that it was going to be difficult getting the body back to the base. But unfortunately, it had to be done. Tired as he was, he helped as the other two began to clear away the snow and ice which had begun to encroach around the dead man. In the process, the fingers that grasped the amulet snapped off and, pocketing it, he continued more cautiously.

Carefully, Chalmers and Kuttner tugged and pried the body out of the compacted shallow grave, raising the frozen arms to drag it completely free. Once done, they hefted it between them and began picking their way through the banks of snow, their eyes always on the lookout for anything that might be lurking in the dense, yet becoming increasingly darker, whiteness, the bright yellow lights of the base leading them on.

Unburdened, Moorcroft led the way, frequently looking over his shoulder to reassure himself that his associates were still behind him. He would then turn swiftly, in order to peer out into the icy wasteland. But there was nothing but the driving snow.

Finally, the three of them reached the base.

Moorcroft banged heavily on the door.

A few seconds later, it opened, and Munro peered out, a wood axe in his hand. He took an unsteady step forward as he caught sight of the rigid body on the ground nearby, half-hidden in shadow and a faint filming of snow. When he saw what it was, he hesitated, then took a sudden, fumbling step backwards even as the professor pushed past him.

Accompanied by a ferocious blast of cold air, Chalmers and Kuttner came inside, Chogan's grim remains supported between them.

Munro closed the door and turned to face them. "What happened?" he asked faintly.

"We don't know," Moorcroft answered. He turned to Chalmers. "What are you going to do with him?"

"There's a small cold storage unit in the basement. I think it best that we put him in there." Chalmers looked around. "Where's Janice?"

"Don't worry, your wife's okay. She's in her room. You know what she's like. She's the only one who's been able to do any work of late," Munro answered.

"Good. Come on, Kuttner, let's get Chogan downstairs before she sees any of this." Heaving the dead weight of the stiff body off the ground, Chalmers, with Kuttner's help, made for the basement.

Moorcroft watched them vanish down the corridor, inwardly hoping that Janice would not appear at an unfortunate moment and witness the grim spectacle. No doubt she would be later informed by her husband. Not wishing to be subjected to Munro's questioning and thinking that he might be of some assistance, he set off after Chalmers and Kuttner.

Heading along the corridor, he passed his room, crossed the small canteen and went to the rear of the base. Beyond an open door was a flight of wooden steps that led down into the storage area. From beyond came the smell of faint diesel fumes and the constant rumbling of the generators which provided electricity to the entire station.

Gingerly, he started down. With each step the temperature plummeted so that by the time he reached the bottom his breath was visible as a frosty mist.

The small, densely cluttered room he entered was lit by a bright fluorescent strip light. All around him were shelves stacked with all the items of hardware required for the running of the station. Oil drums and crates filled with geological drilling tools lay haphazardly in one corner. From beyond the door directly opposite him, he could hear Chalmers and Kuttner bickering.

"Christ, Kuttner. Do you always keep this place in such a bad condition?"

"I've never seen it like this before. It wasn't like this when I checked yesterday morning."

Not wanting to eavesdrop further on their conversation, Moorcroft opened the door and entered the room beyond, almost slipping on the thin sheet of ice which covered the floor.

Both men turned round.

"I'd watch your step in here, professor," warned Chalmers, pointing to the white slickness that covered most of the ground. Icicles hung from the ceiling.

Supporting himself against an oil drum, Moorcroft could see that Chogan had been laid out on top of a worktable in the centre of the room. "Is it normally so cold down here?" he said, shivering.

"No," Chalmers answered. "Before we leave I'll be sure to put the heating up a notch or two."

* * * *

It was only eight o'clock but the weariness of the trek down and then back up the slope had fatigued Moorcroft considerably, so that he was now lying on his bed trying to get to sleep. His light was out and, in the darkness, he turned restlessly, listening to the continuous sound of the storm outside as it gusted relentlessly around the base. If anything it seemed to have become stronger, more savage—almost hurricane-like in strength.

Moorcroft lay in fear, unable to disentangle Chogan's apparently natural death from that horrible thing he had seen the previous night, dreading the scrape of nails against the window or the chanting and the rhythmic beating of drums inside his brain.

Somehow, he managed to drift off.

Sometime later, he stirred out of deep slumber into a room bathed in cold moonlight. All was unusually silent, the wind no longer raging outside. For a time he was disorientated, unsure of his surroundings, unable to anchor himself to reality. And then, he heard it—the noise that had filled his nightmares, the scraping of nails—only this time it was closer, much closer.

It sounded as though it was directly beneath him—under his bed!

It felt as though he had been suddenly plunged into deep, freezing water. Brain-numbing, paralysing terror momentarily stopped his heart. He watched, stricken with fear as in the pale moonlight, a bone-white claw, attached to an almost skeletal arm over which the skin had been stretched taut, crawled over the side of his bed. There came a dreadful shuffling sound as whatever had lain hidden slid out, getting to its feet.

Shaking violently, unable to release the scream that threatened to burst his lungs asunder, he brought his knees up to his chest, cowering away from the grotesque living skeleton that reared before him. Red eyes stared out from a cadaverous, almost mummified face. Black dreadlocks into which beads had been fastened sprouted from its head and around its neck was a necklace of raven feathers and scrimshaw.

Fang-filled mouth opening, it reached forwards, raising its tomahawk, ready to scalp him...

With a violent start, he awoke from his nightmare. His heart was thudding away in his chest and his head was spinning. A cold sweat plastered his hair to his forehead.

Suddenly, there came a loud pounding on his bedroom door.

"Professor!"

Groggily, Moorcroft staggered to his feet and switched on the light, noticing from the wall clock that it had just gone ten. For one terrible moment he thought he was going to see that dreadful being stood, grinning, in the far corner, believing that he was still in his nightmare but thankfully there was nothing there.

"Professor!" The door was thumped again.

"Coming." Moorcroft reached out and opened the door to find Kuttner standing before him. The man looked extremely agitated. "What's going on?"

"Munro's missing!"

"What?" Moorcroft stepped out into the corridor. "Where could he have gone?" he was about to ask something else when he saw Chalmers coming towards them from the canteen, his rifle in his hands.

"You're not going to believe this, but Chogan's gone as well." There was a look of utter bewilderment on Chalmer's face. "His body's not where we left it. The back door's been unlocked so it looks like he's left the base and gone outside. Could be that he wasn't fully dead when we brought him in."

Kuttner swore volubly. "He was dead. There's no doubt about that."

The realisation that he had gone from one nightmare into another struck Moorcroft forcibly. His mind reeled. None of this made any sense. "Surely they can't have gone far in this weather?" he asked.

"I don't know what the hell's happening. Munro's coat and boots are still in his room but as he's nowhere to be found he must be outside somewhere." Chalmers stomped into the lounge and started buttoning up his thick parka.

"I'll come with you," said Moorcroft. "Just give me a minute to get my stuff." He ran back to his room and hastily got into his thermals. He took his heavy coat from where it hung and struggled into it, pulling the fur-lined hood around his face.

Chalmers was already outside by the time he arrived. "Here, take this," he said, handing over a powerful flashlight.

"I'll stay here in case they turn up," said Kuttner.

Together, Chalmers and Moorcroft headed out across the frozen landscape. Swirls of snow fell around them as overhead the aurora borealis played a vibrant, scarlet-green atmospheric lightshow, providing an almost surreal, dark fairy tale backdrop.

It did not take long for them to locate a set of tracks; barefoot prints heading towards where they had left the snowcat.

Panning the flashlight beam straight at it, they were shocked to see shadowy movement inside the small compartment. There was someone—or something—inside.

Gulping back his fear, Moorcroft headed over, Chalmers to one side.

Suddenly the compartment door was thrown open. A blood-spattered thing that had once been Munro leapt down. He looked ghastly; his chalk-white face hollow and sunken, his mouth smeared with gore. In one hand he held a butcher's knife whilst in the other he gripped a severed hand at which he had been gnawing.

"Christ!" shouted Moorcroft. "Shoot him!" he cried as the horror advanced towards them, snarling and drooling hungrily as it came.

"Get back!" Chalmers shouted, raising his rifle. "Get back or I'll fire." His warning fell on deaf ears. And now it was he and the professor who were backing away.

"Shoot him, for God's sake!" Moorcroft shouted.

Chalmers pulled the trigger. Having forgotten to remove the half-bolt safety catch, there came a dull click as the rifle failed to discharge.

And then the blood-covered man before them was changing, dropping to all fours. Bristling, dark grey hair sprouted from his face as his indoor clothes ripped and fell from him. His face elongated, becoming lupine as huge fangs grew from a mouth that was now a maw, a blood-coated muzzle.

Munro had become a wolf, a huge timber wolf, a malign, voracious intelligence in its eyes.

Moorcroft screamed as Chalmers began hastily fumbling with his rifle.

For a moment, the wolf bobbed its massive head from side to side, weighing up its opponents, gauging which of the two men posed the greater threat. Then, with a guttural howl, it expelled a freezing mass of ice and a vapour from its mouth. Glacial motes sparkled within the cloud of rimy breath, Chalmers its target.

Chalmers was quick to react. He leapt to his right, the frosty blast numbing his left-hand side instead of catching him full on. The cold was perishing, almost burning in its ferocity. With a scream of pain, he fell to his knees, dropping his rifle, his right hand gripping his frozen left arm.

The wolf then came at a leap.

Chalmers took its full weight. With a cry, he fell, the huge carnivore on top of him. Frantically, he battered at its snout with a gloved hand, his desperate blows having little effect.

In a savage frenzy, the wolf made to bite down, to tear the flesh from his face.

Chalmers managed to get his right hand in front of its snapping jaws. Three fingers were bitten off and greedily gobbled.

The sudden bang of the rifle going off startled the wolf, causing it to miss what would undoubtedly have been its killing bite. It looked around, its red eyes alive with a cold burning. It saw the other man, the man with the rifle and howled, the sound strangely human. Leaping off its savaged victim, it stalked threateningly towards him, hackles up, belly low to the ground, bluish wisps rising from its muzzle as it began to growl, indicating that it was about to exhale its cloud of freezing death once more.

With the flashlight resting on the snow throwing grotesque shadows, Moorcroft took aim and fired.

The wolf sprang into the air as the high impact bullet struck it in the throat.

Moorcroft shot it a second time and then a third as it limped away into the shadows.

Chalmers staggered over, blood streaming from his wounded hand, a thick coating of frost covering half his body. "Did you kill it?"

"I don't think so but now's not the time to go after it. Wait here." Moorcroft picked up the flashlight, headed over to the snowcat, climbed up and looked inside. Of all the things he had ever seen before this was undoubtedly the worse. Scattered inside were the barely recognisable, gory remains of the now thawed out Chogan. It took only the briefest of glimpses to fill the professor's mind with horror for it was clear that he had been partially devoured and that the thing that had been Munro had been feasting on him.

Bile rose in the professor's gullet. Stomach lurching, he jumped down and vomited.

"What is it?" asked Chalmers through gritted teeth.

Wiping spittle from his mouth, Moorcroft straightened. "It's Chogan. That monster's been eating him. Come on. Let's get back to the base and get your hand seen to."

* * * *

Moorcroft sat by the fire, curiously examining the bone amulet that had belonged to the unfortunate Native American, wondering if it possessed any magic that could be of use against whatever it was that was outside in the dark. If it did, then clearly it hadn't provided its previous owner with any talismanic benefits. That is, unless Chogan *had* died from natural causes. For his corpse, prior to having been found mutilated in the snowcat, had borne no sign of external violence.

Alongside his wife, Chalmers sat shivering nearby, sullenly staring into his steaming coffee, his right hand heavily bandaged; the frost that had coated him had melted away, sloughing off like a snake's skin. He was in constant pain however and having changed into dry clothes, they had all been shocked to see the blackened, almost frostbitten skin beneath.

Armed with the rifle, Kuttner was on patrol in addition to making desperate attempts to make radio contact.

The weather outside was atrocious. Cold, white death blasted at the base and despite Moorcroft's best efforts to regulate the inside heating it was steadily becoming colder.

Equally alarming was the way in which the lights constantly flickered, threatening to go out at any moment. The last thing they needed was for them to be plunged into icy darkness—a darkness, Moorcroft was certain, in which he would then see those malevolent red eyes. Consequently, he had the flashlight nearby.

"Chogan was right," Chalmers muttered, deliriously. "It is the Wendigo. And what's more it isn't going to let any of us leave here."

Janice looked worriedly at her husband. She was the trained medic and although she had treated and cleaned his wound with alcohol and Betadine, it was still quite possible that it had become infected. She knew he seriously needed hospital attention.

Chalmers' eyes were wide and staring. "I'm telling you, it's going to kill us all. And then it's going to eat us."

Moorcroft had heard enough. Rising to his feet, he went in search of Kuttner, hoping against hope that he would find the other speaking into the radio, having made contact with the outside world. Instead, he found him exiting the lavatories.

"How's Chalmers doing?" Kuttner asked.

"To be honest with you, I can't see him making it through the night," Moorcroft answered truthfully. "As things currently stand, I don't see any of us making it through the night," he added.

"I still can't believe what you told us about Munro. Are you sure he turned into a wolf?"

Moorcroft nodded.

"And are you sure you didn't kill him? I mean, if you say you shot him three times with this," Kuttner held up the rifle, "then I can't see how—" He was interrupted by a violent swirl of wind that rocked the entire base.

With a loud crash, the heavy rear exit door which had been securely bolted smashed open and an icy gale howled along the corridor, buffeting the two men as they turned in that direction, almost knocking them off their feet. Their eyes stung. A thin layer of frost instantly formed on their faces.

A tumultuous blizzard swept down the corridor with stunning force.

When it cleared, moments later, Moorcroft heard that dreadful mournful chanting accompanied by that frenzied drumming inside his head.

Stood in the wrecked doorway, illuminated by a swinging strip light which looked as though it was about to fall from its mooring at any moment, was that horribly tall, practically skeletal, fiend—that hideous aberration of a Native American shaman. Shadows danced weirdly around it.

Stooping slightly, brandishing its tomahawk, it stepped inside, red eyes glaring.

Kuttner screamed and brought his hands to his ears. "Make it stop! For the love of God, make it stop!" Thick red blood began trickling between his fingers. He then began flailing at the air as though he were trying to shake off an attack from an invisible raven.

Moorcroft knew that for some reason—perhaps due to the powers of the amulet he had in his trouser pocket—the terrible noise wasn't affecting him anywhere near as badly. Scrambling for the rifle, he flicked off the safety, took aim and squeezed the trigger. He missed and the bullet ricocheted against the far wall. He was about to shoot a second time when, with a violent belch, the horror projected a thick stream of vaporous liquid from its mouth.

The super cold regurgitation blasted into Kuttner, striking him like liquid nitrogen. He crystallised almost instantly.

Then, to Moorcroft's revulsion, parts of the research student broke away.

Frozen chunks of solid man crashed to the floor of the passage. Little bloody ice floes separating from the main iceberg.

Something seemed to snap in Moorcroft's brain. A shrieking insanity tugged fiercely at his mind, rising like a dark tide which threatened to engulf him, to bury him beneath its dark waters from which there was no escape.

There then came a loud crash directly behind him as the stretch of interconnecting passage which joined the canteen and the bedrooms with the main lounge caved in. Sudden, freezing wind and snow gusted in through the rent opening. Throughout the base, the lights flickered, dimmed and then went out.

Something had struck the professor on the head and in the darkness, he could feel what he assumed was blood trickling down his face. Taking the flashlight from his pocket, he flicked it on, dreading what he might see. He winced, noticing the shattered remains of Kuttner, not fully able to come to terms with the fact that this scattered pile of icy blue and red matter had once been a living being. It was a truly obscene way to die. Still, there was no sign of the monster—the Wendigo, as Chogan had called it.

He knew that he had to get proper shelter before he froze to death. Teeth chattering, well aware that he couldn't go back the way he had come, Moorcroft headed around the base to the front entrance, the beam from his flashlight throwing horrible shadows that seemed to shift of their own volition. The main door was wide open.

"Chalmers!" he shouted. His hands were shaking, and his hair and eyebrows had become rimed with frost. He had lost all feeling in his toes.

There was no answer.

Shakily, Moorcroft entered, his flashlight in one hand, rifle in the other.

Bile rose to his gullet upon seeing the sight before him.

Crouched by the body of her husband, munching away at his bloody, torn open corpse, was Janice Chalmers—or rather the vile entity that now possessed her. She turned, hissing her displeasure at this intrusion, her snow-white face smeared with gore. Bloody hands which clenched the wrist at which she had been chewing, swung up to her red eyes in order to shield them from the beam of light.

Dropping the flashlight, Moorcroft raised the rifle and fired. The recoil jarred along his frozen limbs as the bullet blasted away a portion of the ghoul's head, knocking it back. He fired again, blowing a hole in the thing's chest.

With an unearthly screech, the thing began to shape-change.

The clothes it wore shredded and fell away as grey-brown fur erupted all over its body. Its face lengthened, becoming a fang-filled maw, a thick, shaggy mane around its neck. Hands became massive, clawed paws.

Snarling, its metamorphosis now complete, the huge grizzly bear lumbered to its feet, its head brushing the ceiling.

Moorcroft sobbed with fear and horror, letting the useless rifle clatter to the ground. He knew he could not withstand an attack from this monster but raised his arms involuntarily, to block the terrible beast. A moment later the bear was on him, slashing with its claws, but they passed, ineffectually, straight through him. The creature bellowed with rage and frustration.

Galvanised by the bear's seeming inability to hurt him, Moorcroft scrambled backwards, away from it. He turned and ran, dashing headlong into the freezing night, floundering desperately through the thick snow, his mind and body temporarily oblivious to the cold such was his fear. The raging insanity of all he had seen obliterated his sanity and he was aware only of the adrenaline flooding him and the dreadful roars echoing through the night.

* * * *

The day after the snowstorm had ended, a small Mountain Rescue team had come from Wrigley to check on the geological station and see why none of their radio messages had been answered. The three men had got over the heavy snow by dog sled and were making their way up the slopes to the base. The snow had piled in drifts against trees and the going was slow and careful. One drift near the station was larger than the others and as a section of snow slipped down, they could see a flash of yellow underneath.

"That must be the snowcat," their leader commented. "Strange to find it over here. They normally keep it right by the station." He used a long pole to brush more of the snow off, uncovering the windscreen.

All three men jumped as there came a shriek from inside the cabin of the vehicle.

"Jesus, there's someone in there! Quickly, get the snow off this thing."

The shrieking continued as they worked, shovelling the snow away from the vehicle's door.

"Nearly there...done it!" The leader levered open the door and then recoiled in shock.

The interior of the cabin was spattered with gory remains—all that was left of Chogan. Huddled in one corner, stinking and dishevelled, was Moorcroft. His eyes were wide in terror and his clothes and face were smeared with blood.

"You can't eat me!" he giggled, brandishing a small bone amulet. The rescuers fell back in horror from the raving, wild-eyed man as he continued to shriek, his voice tipping further into hysteria. "You killed the others, but *you can't eat me!* YOU CAN'T EAT ME!"

The men looked at each other in dawning horror, taking in the lunatic before them and the just discernibly human remains he was squatting amongst and then, at a nod from their leader, the two youngest started off towards the geological station, dreading what they would find within.